The Best-Laid Plans

A Maps and Chipper Adventure

David Gubbins.

david.gubbins@talk21.com

David Gubbins

Strategic Book Publishing and Rights Co.

Strategic Book Publishing & Rights Co., LLC
USA | Singapore
www.sbpra.net

For information about special discounts for bulk purchases, please contact Strategic Book Publishing and Rights Co. Special Sales, at bookorder@sbpra.net.

ISBN: 978-1-68235-315-8

The Best-Laid Plans

Dedicated to:

Christian
Shirley
Brenda
John

The Secret Is Out

Did we design it to fail, or did we fail to design it?

In a field not far from the factory lay the remains of a prototype aeroplane. Splinters of wood lay strewn across the ploughed field, and an engine hung precariously in the branches of a nearby tree. The cows that occupied the field where smoke now rose gazed at it with contempt.

The idea was sound: a large aeroplane that could transport soldiers anywhere on the front where they were needed. The execution, however, wasn't so sound. Built from wood and fabric, the aeroplane initially performed as well as could have been expected, but this flight was the first with any kind of internal load. The twenty pounds of clothing conservatively placed over the main wing spar had tipped the balance, and now the clothing smoldered with the rest of the once magnificent aeroplane.

It was indeed fortunate that no one was hurt when the aeroplane failed to take off and ploughed through several hedges, colliding with the trees that lined the field.

After months of building, testing and redesigning, the aircraft looked the part. Its four engines perched over its lower wing were deemed to have enough power for the job. The wings had been carefully designed to provide the lift necessary for the task. The tail surfaces were deemed to offer sufficient directional stability. Yet here it was, crashed and burned in a field.

The two pilots had extricated themselves from the wreck and were sitting near a gate shivering with shock. It hadn't taken long for the scientists and boffins to arrive at the crash site. The scene that met them was shocking. Their first thought was for the pilots; when they were found an ambulance was called and the two men were rushed to the nearest hospital, which was located at the recently founded flying school.

As the scientists doused the smoldering remains, the horse-drawn ambulance arrived at the scene. The ambulance staff coaxed the two men in the cart and they were rushed away to the sick quarters at the local flying school. Finding a queue of young men waiting to be shown into the hospital, the ambulance driver ran into the hospital intent on finding some staff.

He was greeted by a young nurse; her pressed and pristine uniform was a sight to behold. As the ambulance driver looked at the young nurse and drew a long breath, the nurse looked past him to see the patients still sitting on the cart. Her eyes widened and her professional tone became more curt. The driver once more tried to grab her attention, but even as the nurse surveyed the situation the driver found her impossible to ignore. The driver spluttered out his purpose, finding words somewhat difficult to come by, his incoherent tone and garbled sentences failing to impress the nurse. With one more breath and a manic gesture he finally got her attention.

Victoria hadn't been a nurse for long. Brought up in a privileged family who frowned upon her quest to help in the war effort, she fought to get where she was, convinced of her notion that the war couldn't possibly be won by men alone. Now confronted by the first real casualty she had been confronted with, she leapt into action.

A doctor was called, space in the treatment room was found and nurses who were normally friends and colleagues were ordered to get the line of potential patients out of the way.

Several hundred feet away, in a quiet corner of the dining hall, two young men in uniform were tucking into their morning oat cereal. Neither were particularly enamoured with their breakfast fare but they were both determined to eat something before the day commenced. Charles Edward Medlicott, known universally as Maps due to his incredible sense of direction and navigation skills, held his nose and chewed the mixture as best he could; he had tasted worse. Maps had joined up in the first wave of recruits to the Army and, after spending several months in the trenches of France, he volunteered for aerial duties with the flying corps. A tall, striking-looking gentleman, Maps was dedicated to his job spending long hours studying maps of the local area, picking out landmarks and other observable features.

Since arriving at the flying school Maps had teamed up with Michael McGraw. Michael was the son of a ship's carpenter and had become widely known as Chipper, a nickname he actually rather liked.

Chipper had recently been subject to military discipline and, as a consequence, spent many hours peeling potatoes in the dining hall. This morning he found half an hour to spend with Maps and was determined to enjoy the time.

Chipper also regarded his breakfast with distain. He was used to an oat breakfast in the morning; however, he preferred more milk and found the half-cooked oats to be less than the warm, tasty breakfast his father used to cook. Still, he forced himself to eat, washing down each mouthful with the lukewarm coffee he was served.

Chipper joined the flying corps directly from his civilian carpentry job and was still learning the ways and the foibles of the military. His hand-eye coordination was considered exceptional, a talent he used to promote himself as a pilot. With Maps in the back of the aeroplane, he and Chipper made a fine aerial team and the two were encouraged to fly as much as possible together, the powers that be seeing them as a single unit rather than two individuals.

In spite of his exceptional hand-eye coordination skills, Chipper wasn't comfortable when not using his talent. He often found himself being involved in silly accidents due to his clumsy and skittish behaviour. It was during one of these silly accidents that he first met Victoria. He burnt his hand on a tea urn on a winter's morning and was sent to the medical quarters for treatment. Like most of the men in the training school, he found himself unavoidable attracted to Victoria. It was Chipper who introduced Victoria to Maps and the three of them had become very close friends.

Espionage

The crash of the aeroplane had awoken the inhabitants of the local market town. Indeed, Arnold woke with quite a start!

The enormous noise of the crash had thrown him from his bed. The noise made the teacups rattle in his cupboards, the pictures fall from the walls and caused the curtains in the bedroom to sway casting an eerie sunlight around the room. Arnold rubbed his eyes, picked himself up from the floor and looked at his watch. It was seven-thirty in the morning!

Arnold was a pseudonym; his real name was Sebastian. He had taken the name Arnold after arriving on these shores, naming himself after the first shop he had seen in the high street. Born in continental Europe, he had been residing in England for some time; his passage to England was undertaken in the care of the crew of a deeply uncomfortable submarine. His sponsors in a foreign land had prepared him for life in England, teaching him to sound and behave as they thought an Englishman would behave. There appeared to have been little left to chance; the clothes, the mannerism and the quirky little phrases had been meticulously worked on and perfected. Arnold's work was of the utmost importance to his government.

He settled into the local community that had recently become a hub of aviation activity thanks to a network of friends in an area. A flying school nearby had seen a large influx of young men and women in the area, and this once sleepy and largely ignored little corner of the country was now considered to be a bustling and active market town.

Apart from the occasional rude awakening, Arnold was content to do his work and enjoy the surroundings of a quiet existence in the English countryside. The tools of his trade, his eyes and ears, had already supplied his masters with invaluable information on the amount of preparations that were being carried out. The noise that awoke him so rudely was of great interest to him, as anything unusual in the area was prone to do.

By mid-morning, Arnold had done all the things that foreign agents would normally do, picking up the milk and the newspapers, soon he was ready for a day of nosing around. Espionage was an easy job in those days, he would recall many years later. The British seemed to grumble about foreigners more than worry about their activities. The war that was raging was in some foreign land, many miles from their towns and cities. Their young men cheerfully marched off to the continent to fight in what appeared to be a blissful ignorance of the trouble they were getting themselves into.

Blessed as he was with a talent for languages and mimicry, Arnold often mused that if he told everyone in the local ale house that he wasn't English they would undoubtedly laugh at him. Confident of the impregnable nature of their island, the English, indeed the British, carried on their lives as if nothing was happening in the world.

The war was now into its second year and not a lot had changed in this part of England. The people carried on their daily lives, grumbling and moaning about shortages in the shops and queuing for practically everything. The grumbling and moaning allowed Arnold to integrate quite comfortably. His sponsors had spent many hours teaching and evaluating his skills in this area.

The lack of a young male population was the only noticeable difference to the pre-war life he remembered in his homeland.

Arnold grabbed a light jacket and headed to the local market. As he joined a queue of people waiting to buy root vegetables, he listened and noted anything of importance that was said. The absence of the nice young bank clerk or the performance of the local football team would normally have been unremarkable, but Arnold noted it and took it as an indication of the number of men who were going to war. Arriving at the front of the queue, the store holder asked him if he had been awoken by the noise that morning.

"Of course, I had," Arnold grumbled. "The noise was enormous. It damned near shook the house to pieces."

"Heh!" said the store holder. "Come a little closer."

Arnold leaned over the few parsnips that were artfully arranged on the stand, edging ever closer to the store holder.

"I reckon that that was our new secret aeroplane." the store holder casually explained. "Talk is that it crashed in the woods early this morning."

"Really," replied the foreign agent.

"Oh aye, local gossip has it that it is a really big aeroplane, loads of engines and enough space to fit a small army inside! Those boffins you see in the pubs around here are building it on the airfield in the woods." Proud of his gossip, the store holder slipped an extra carrot into the paper bag full of parsnips, and with a practiced flip of the wrist, the bag was closed.

"Sixpence, please!" The deal was done, and dinner was in the bag.

Arnold returned to his house to drop off his dinner. The storekeeper's words kept going around in his head. Finding a map that he had hidden carefully under the kitchen table he looked for a suitable spot for an airfield in a local wood. An area of green caught his eye—a long stretch of wood, parted down the middle. It looked ideal. The wood was called Secret Wood. Arnold may have unwittingly stumbled upon the secret aeroplane, manufactured in a secret factory … in secret wood.

That evening as the sun was setting, Arnold walked the couple of miles or so to the Secret Wood, and after looking around, to make sure that the coast was clear, he slipped into the trees. His attempts to avoid broken twigs from cracking under his feet were useless. It was fortunate that the wood appeared to be uninhabited and strangely silent. Fearing he had wasted his time, Arnold resolved to walk deeper into the woods for only another five minutes. If nothing caught his attention, he would then turn around and reassess his options. His progress was suddenly halted by a stern shouted command.

"Who goes there? Friend or foe?" the voice bellowed.

Now Arnold was a clever sort, and he knew that there would be a right answer to this question and a wrong answer. As a soldier appeared from behind a tree, Arnold knew he had only one option.

"Friend," he replied.

"Oh, that's okay then," the soldier replied dropping his tone. The soldier lowered his rifle and he walked forward, relieved that after hours of tedious guarding here was a person he could talk to.

"What brings you out this way?" the guard inquired.

"I have lost my dog," Arnold replied. "A small black dog, and he's my only companion. I think he went that way." Arnold pointed in the direction from where the guard appeared.

"Well, you can't go through there," the guard explained. "The government's top scientists and engineers are building a huge secret aeroplane over there."

"Scientists and engineers?" Arnold enquired.

"Yes, you know boffin-type people in white coats, carrying clipboards."

Arnold hung on every word the soldier spoke. The two men chatted for a while before exhausting the conversation.

"Your dog hasn't returned," The soldier noted.

Arnold, reminded of his dog, implored the soldier to let him through his guard post.

"Can't do that. It would be wrong," the soldier explained. "But if you walk about two hundred yards farther, there is a gap in the fence. You can get through there."

Arnold thanked the guard and assured him that he wouldn't tell a soul about the conversation. Before picking up his rifle once more and returning to his post, the guard expressed his hope that Arnold would find his little dog.

Encouraged by this new information, Arnold walked two hundred yards farther into the woods where he found the gap; a slightly rickety old stile spanned the rusting and ancient-looking barbed wire fence. Arnold strode confidently over the stile, then as a familiar sense of foreboding embraced him, he carefully forded a stream and approached the field.

In front of him was a huge aeroplane, as big an aeroplane as Arnold had ever seen. Its beautiful white cylindrical fuselage reflected the red glow of the descending sun. Attached to the fuselage were mounted two enormous sets of wings, a biplane arrangement at the rear and a triplane arrangement at the front. The tail appeared to be a multifaceted arrangement of horizontal and vertical pieces. The whole aeroplane was trussed together with wires, giving the aeroplane the appearance of an exceptionally large musical instrument. Lying atop the forward wings were four huge engines complete with unfeasibly large propellers. The rear wings housed an equally large number of engines driving equally large propellers.

Arnold carefully approached the aeroplane, and after creeping along the length of it, he found that the cylindrical fuselage tapered elegantly to a needlepoint nose. On the opposite side of the aeroplane was a large door cut into the side of the fuselage and hinged at the top. The door was propped open with a large metal prop that held it firmly in this position. The open door afforded Arnold ready access to the aeroplane's cavernous interior. The opportunity was too good to miss, so Arnold boldly climbed aboard the aeroplane.

Seats were mounted along the walls of the fuselage. He counted each of them and determined that this machine would be capable of carrying at least twenty-five people. Arnold's background in engineering made him wonder how on earth an aeroplane this big would ever get airborne, so he pushed his luck a little and clambered into the cockpit. Large comfortable seats cushioned him as he seated himself at the controls. The cockpit was enclosed, yet the windows offered a superb view of the outside world. Looking over his shoulder, he studied the engines. They were quite obviously powerful and appeared to be fed fuel from large tanks built into the wing above each engine. The sheer bulk of the aeroplane made Arnold skeptical that it could fly.

Suddenly Arnold became aware of movement in the rear of the aeroplane and turned to see a guard, a guard he hadn't seen before, with a gun, looking at him with a startled expression.

"What are you doing in there?" the guard asked.

Arnold stuttered momentarily before he blurted out as good an excuse as he could imagine. "I am looking for my dog," he explained. "You haven't seen a little black dog around here have you?"

The guard hadn't seen a dog that day, and after grasping Arnold by the collar, he hauled him away to the main building on the site, where he was offered a nice cup of tea. The guard poured himself a cup of tea and the two men chatted about dogs for the next twenty minutes or so. On the hour the guard was changed. The soldier that was coming off duty was the man Arnold had seen in the woods. He also poured himself some tea and joined Arnold at the table.

"Did you find your dog?" the guard inquired.

"No, he must be miles away by now, I honestly thought he had jumped into your aeroplane."

The guard agreed that the dog could indeed have jumped into the aeroplane. "He likes doing that sort of thing," Arnold explained.

The guard felt concerned for the little dog and, believing Arnold to be an honest sort of bloke, he ushered Arnold out of the building with instructions to find that dog. Arnold left the building somewhat relieved, and he melted away into the woods.

That evening Arnold sat up late writing up notes on what he had seen. His detailed description of the aeroplane would doubtless spur his masters into action. All he had to do was keep his ear close to the ground and wait for action, or instructions. His dreams that night were full of the heroic adventures that he could have in the woods trying to destroy the secret aeroplane, or aeroplanes.

Early the next morning Arnold took a bus to the coast and at the appointed hour he cast the case full of intelligence into the sea, where a swimmer retrieved it and swam back to a submarine, which shortly afterwards descended elegantly below the waves.

Arnold watched the submarine's disappearance with satisfaction. He was sure that he had done his country a great service that day.

Courtship

In the three months since Victoria had started to work as a nurse in the sick quarters, the morning sick parade has become an increasingly popular meeting place. The men at the school, having had little if any female contact for what seemed an eternity, seemed to have developed all manner of illnesses and ailments. Most of the nurses saw that this was any excuse for them to get the tall and elegant Victoria alone in a room. Victoria was highly intelligent but had a rather sheltered upbringing. She found it difficult to understand why the other nurses giggled at her naivety. Victoria just got on with things as best she could, her cool and professional manner befitting her status as the nursing team leader.

The commander of the school was not so tall and certainly lacked that element of elegance that Victoria wore so well. He was keenly aware of his role as a commander, a role he took incredibly seriously. His routine was timed to the second and woe betide anyone that put him off kilter. He tried to know everyone under his command; he tried to understand all their roles and their importance in the structure of the team that he oversaw. He believed that he had no favourites and treated everyone with the respect they earned and deserved. Discipline was key to the success of his school and he hoped that all around him his instructors and pupils were team players all driven toward the same goal. Deep down, however, he knew that as long as there was food in the dining halls and activity enough for the students, the school would actually run itself.

For a month or so, something was nagging at him. His beliefs, at first, refused to let him comprehend it, but it became too obvious to ignore. There was a bout of absenteeism in his school. The dining halls were checked and found sufficiently stocked; therefore, the activities for the men were obviously lacking. Having seen no aeroplanes on the line that morning, he resolved that action would have to be taken.

Arriving at his desk, he was mortified to find his usual cup of tea absent. He called for his trusted batman intent on getting to the bottom of this outrageous omission from his daily routine. The batman failed to answer the call. The secretary, however, was only too pleased to inform the commander that the batman had gone sick.

"Damned nuisance," cursed the commander. "I will have to take the dog for a walk this morning!"

The dog stirred in his basket on hearing the word "walk," his tail wagging he approached the commander. The commander patted the mutt gently on its head, grabbed his leash and, after attaching the leash to the collar, the pair headed for the door.

"Seems that everyone is sick," the secretary commented.

Before he and his dog left the office, he asked the secretary to get someone from the sick quarters to his office – someone who could give him an explanation for the absenteeism, by the time he returned.

"I will get to the bottom of this this!" the commander muttered as the door slammed behind him.

The secretary, who was as efficient as ever, was only too pleased to carry out the commander's orders.

Victoria was the lead nurse on duty that morning. As a conscientious nurse she had been charged that morning, as most mornings to be fair, with attending to an endless queue of young men complaining of pains here and aches there. Victoria wondered how the small medical team managed to cope prior to her arrival. On hearing the ring of the telephone, she looked around and finding herself alone she excused herself and took the call.

The secretary asked her to report to the commander at once.

"It's the morning sick parade," Victoria answered. "And I have a line of sick men queuing out of the door along with two injured pilots from the crash this morning. I can't report anywhere at the moment!"

The secretary insisted, and Victoria reluctantly accepted that she would have to leave her post and go.

"Oh bother," she sighed.

Looking around she found a colleague sipping a large cup of tea.

"Can you deal with the queue?" she asked. "The old man wants to see me immediately."

The colleague grumbled a little, the unfairness of it all being upmost in here mind. Duty was important however, and as the "old man" was calling, the colleague reluctantly agreed to take over.

Victoria grabbed her cape and threw it around her shoulders as she made for the door.

The men growled and grumbled as Victoria swept passed. The colleague appeared and summoned the first young man in the queue. On seeing Victoria's colleague, the men growled and grumbled some more. The men at the back craned their necks to see who had taken over. After weighing up the possibility of Victoria returning, most gave up and slowly went back to work.

Arriving at the commander's office, the secretary offered Victoria a cup of tea and asked her to wait for the commander's return. Victoria accepted the kind offer and after removing her heavy cape, she sat on the chair by the window and awaited the return of the commander.

It was several minutes before the door opened and in ran a small dog, followed by the commander. The dog enthusiastically greeted Victoria, who was balancing her hot tea in one hand while trying to fend off the attentions of the dog with the other. The dog persisted, jumping at Victoria with enthusiasm until the commander told the dog in no uncertain terms to lie down.

The commander asked Victoria to follow him into his office where he offered her the seat on the opposite side of the desk. Victoria politely accepted and straightened her long, ankle-length skirt before she settled into the seat.

The commander explained the problem and asked for an opinion.

"I simply cannot get aeroplanes on the airfield in a fit state for the pilots to fly …" he started before adding, "whatever plague is afflicting these men needs to be diagnosed, and quickly!"

Victoria replied that the sick quarters had become so overcrowded that it was taking a little time to process the patients. She added that she was most surprised at the number of sick men she had to deal with every day.

"Well, exactly how many of my staff are ill?" the commander barked. He was not at all happy.

"This morning I have counted forty-eight, sir," Victoria replied.

"And the nature of this ailment, young lady?" the commander enquired, showing his determination to get to the bottom of this mystery.

"Well, to be honest, I haven't found a single one with any ailment at all," Victoria explained.

"None!"

"Well, to be fair, one had a slight scratch over his right eye."

"Slight scratch? Were there any serious injuries this morning? Something like flu or gout, or just all scratches, poorly tired legs and exhaustion?"

Victoria could only confirm the commander's worst fears.

"Is it just the men?" he asked. "Or are the flyers joining in as well?"

Victoria confirmed that the ailment had affected all ranks and positions.

"Are you quite sure they aren't turning up to spend some time with you?"

"Why would they want to do that?" Victoria naively asked.

She had absolutely no idea of the effect she was having on the men of the flying school. Men were falling over themselves to see her. Normally conscientious workers, the type that would never have taken a day off sick, were finding themselves drawn to the morning sick parades. The commander was well aware of the effect Victoria was having on both his troops and himself.

"I would like to discuss this with you right now, but I have a school to run. Perhaps you would be good enough to join me for dinner this evening?"

The commander had little doubt that Victoria would accept his invitation. Few refused his company and after all Victoria needed to make friends, and what better friend could a nurse have than her commander.

"I am busy this evening, sir. I have arranged to have dinner with two pilots this evening," Victoria explained.

"Busy?" the commander choked. "Which two pilots might they be?"

"Maps Medlicott and Chipper McGraw," explained Victoria.

"I see," the commander said. Medlicott and McGraw weren't unknown to him. They had recently been involved in a very nasty incident with Victoria and her father.

"Does your father know about this?" the commander asked.

Victoria wondered what on earth her father had to do with the subject. It was just a little something to eat with a couple of friends.

"Don't you know that student pilots fraternizing with nurses is strictly not allowed in this school?" the commander said interrupting Victoria's thought process.

"We aren't fraternizing!" Victoria exclaimed. "We are simply having something to eat together."

The commander felt it necessary at this point to explain that these pilots were a long way from home and sometimes in those circumstances, a man's intentions are sometimes far from being gentlemanly.

"That is why I forbid fraternizing between young nurses and pilots," the commander explained.

"But commanders can fraternize to their hearts content?" replied an annoyed Victoria.

"Commanders and pilots are two completely different entities," the commander further explained. "Besides," he added, "High Command has noticed a drop in the number of hours this school has been flying and as these Maps and Chipper fellows are the only two fit pilots I appear to have, I need them to go flying."

The commander was correct, in the last month there had been a 75 percent drop in the number of flying hours, mainly due to the men reporting sick. The consequence of this was that aeroplanes would only be available to fly when the men had recovered from their various ailments and generated an aeroplane that was fit to fly. That would only occur later in the day, the evening for example. He added that he couldn't send one of the sick pilots, as that could endanger a perfectly good aeroplane.

Maybe the commander felt this was sufficient justification for his decision, but he also knew that it was his wife's evening out with friends; therefore, there would be no hindrance to his gallivanting around with this nurse.

"Oh bother," muttered the nurse. "They will be so disappointed. I've had to cancel dinner with them on two previous occasions."

"I will send my car to pick you up at about eight, if that's all right with you."

"I suppose so," Victoria replied with little enthusiasm.

Victoria made her excuses and turned to leave the office saddened that this wasn't the last time she would see of the commander that day.

Student Pilots

Maps and Chipper retired to the small tent that they called home. A pleasant enough bolt hole but hardly the sort of place anyone would willingly live in. Maps maintained his side of the tent in immaculate condition. His uniforms were all clean and pressed, hanging from the wardrobe ready for wearing at a moment's notice. His shoes were all sitting at the bottom of the wardrobe; all were highly polished. Maps liked to have things ready and could be obsessive about their place in the wardrobe.

Chipper considered Maps's tidiness a little odd. He failed to match the high standards set by his friend. Whilst he was suffering the vagaries of military discipline, he cleverly converted his bed into an ironing board. This had rather awkwardly resulted in him having to sleep on the floor amongst the tins of shoe polish and numerous cloths he had used to apply it. Maps would often casually kick these cloths under the bed when they encroached into his area. Chipper found this behaviour more than a little annoying but understood that Maps needed his living space to be tidy.

Recently his daily routine had been reduced to shuttling between the kitchen to peel potatoes, the airfield to fly, and the tent he shared with Maps to rest. What little time he had to himself was spent polishing shoes, ironing uniforms, and presenting himself for inspection as and when required by senior ranks. Chipper found it all so pointless but through the encouragement of the much more experienced Maps, he soon learned to play their little game.

Fortunately his period of discipline had come to a sudden and abrupt end that morning. He had jumped through all the hoops that he had been presented with. He served his time and was now deemed to be adequate service person. The resentment he felt at such a silly game was a little more difficult to shake off. Maps spent much time getting Chipper through the disciplinary process and both were agreed that a repeat wouldn't happen, at least at this establishment.

For the first time in months Chipper found he had a moment to himself and so, leaving Maps to tidy up the things he last tidied up twenty minutes ago, he wandered outside and sat for a moment in the bright morning sun.

In the sunshine Chipper's thoughts turned to his future. He had fallen behind in his studies, a fact that kept him awake at night further hindering his studies. His piloting skills were to a certain extent a natural talent borne of his incredible balance and reactions. Talent in this field was, however, not exactly recognized. Flying being such a new occupation, the required skills were taught with minute detail.

The science behind flying required study that was little understood by both teachers and pilots; both seemed to combine to cobble together an explanation that made some sort of sense. Sadly, the piloting was only one aspect of his life, however much he enjoyed it. He was forever grateful that Maps was around to help him with his navigation skills. The two men helped each other, and they had grown remarkably close throughout the course.

Presently Maps joined him, bringing the promise of a little conversation.

"Would you care to join us this evening?" Maps asked.

"Join you?" Chipper replied.

"Victoria and I are having dinner in the village this evening. She rather hoped you would join us."

Chipper was flattered that Victoria asked for him to join them and gladly accepted. At any other time the chatter would have been about their evening dinner date; however, at this hour of the day Chipper decided it was time to confide in his friend and discuss the problems he was having at the school. Maps, who was desperate to chat about dinner, decided that his friend needed help.

Chipper was only too pleased to explain his deep-seated concerns about his studies. He explained that since his unfortunate flight with Victoria, and his incarceration in the kitchen for the month that followed, he had resolved to take a leaf from Maps's book.

"My book?"

Chipper explained that Maps was so well respected around the school, and he felt that was because Maps had studied navigation so diligently. The instructors and students very rarely see their star student Maps without a chart in his hand, or at a desk marking angles and distances on the charts. Chipper explained that if he were to progress any, he would need to be as diligent in his studies as Maps was.

"Now you are playing the game!" Maps, the battle-hardened veteran that he pretended he was, said cheerily.

Maps explained that although he was often found with charts and angles, he really didn't know what he was doing. However, the instructors would be more likely to give information to a student that was seen to be interested than a student that just wanted to get through the course. Maps failed to mention that he secretly admired the piloting skills of his friend.

"I see," Chipper said. "But you do know what you are doing. You have never been lost!"

Maps rather pompously explained that was due to more sinking in than it would to a less capable student. In truth his memory was more than often jogged by the features he had seen on the ground and the way those features related to the symbology he had seen gazing down upon a chart. His success in navigation was, therefore, more a product of his visual acuity than his study.

"That is my point exactly," Chipper yelped. "The more I get familiar with the illustrations and diagrams in the books, the more I can connect that with the dials and levers in the cockpit."

"Precisely," Maps congratulated his friend. "That gives us both more time to spend in the village with Victoria and her friends."

"Friends?" a worried Chipper asked.

"Yes friends, you can't expect her to come along on her own, do you?"

Chipper thought for a moment and agreed that Victoria on her own would be an uncomfortable threesome. "A few friends will be a great opportunity for us both to meet more people."

Maps indeed believed that to be the case. Victoria had already kissed him politely on the cheek, a gesture Maps had interpreted as a positive. A few more friends around the table may afford him the opportunity to study this wonderfully attractive young nurse, safe in the knowledge that Chipper would be more than enough distraction for Victoria's friends. The using of his friends in this manner wasn't a side of Maps that Maps liked a great deal, but he knew he had to deal with his feelings for Victoria whilst she still appeared to be encouraging him. Besides the die had been cast, and the pilot seemed none the worse for agreeing to plans of his navigator.

Having spent probably too long chatting, Maps and Chipper made their way over to the flight office where they could continue studies in the large wooden shack that had been erected entirely for the purpose of planning flights.

Nurses

Shortly before lunch Maps and Chipper received the commander's tasking note. They were to fly a practice patrol to the north and the east of the airfield, in an area bounded by the sea to the east and the large river to the north. The note stressed that the exercise should be planned to take no less than two hours and no more than four, in which time they were expected to have covered a minimum of two hundred miles. The journey should be photographed enroute for inspection by the instructor upon their return.

As they both studied the note, it became increasingly obvious to them that they would never get the task done before they were due to meet Victoria and her friends. Chipper studied the route with a sense of deep resentment, offering the opinion that he could through a little cheating, shorten the route to accommodate the two men's social engagement. Maps reminded him that it was their duty to complete the task as planned, besides there would be other days.

"Remember, it's all a game," Maps reminded his friend.

Chipper reluctantly agreed that it would be in their best interests to complete the task properly. He failed, however, to understand why the rules always changed and the goalposts always moved.

Maps and Chipper were discussing who should tell Victoria when the door to the flight planning room opened and there she stood. Both men stood to greet her and invite her inside. Chipper took the nurse's coat and Maps ushered her to a comfortable seat by the map table. He perched himself on the arm of her chair.

"It looks like Chipper and I will be flying later this evening. It seems the commander has some kind of bee in his bonnet about our flying hours," Maps explained.

"Yes, I heard," Victoria replied. "The commander told me all about it when he was inviting me for dinner this evening."

"The commander is taking you for dinner?" questioned Chipper whilst fumbling with the kettle under a hot tap.

Victoria explained the situation as best she could, making it as obvious as she could that she would have preferred to be out with Maps and Chipper rather than the commander. "The commander has spoken, however, and I have no reason to refuse." She already made her mind up that she would make this unwelcome dinner as uncomfortable for the commander as she could.

"You could always go sick," Maps told her. "We won't be back too late this evening."

"I would love to," Victoria replied. "The nurses and all of the others were so looking forward to an evening out."

"Others?" questioned Maps.

Victoria explained that there would be several of the men, the nurses had met over the past few weeks, coming along.

Maps moved uneasily about, the gravity of the situation was immediately obvious to him. It was with a very heavy heart that he accepted the situation.

"Is the tea ready?" he asked.

Chipper finished making hot tea for the three of them. He wasn't as disappointed as Maps but still, after so long in the kitchen and on the parade ground, he longed for the company of friends. "Yes, tea is ready," he announced carrying the large teapot over to the table.

Victoria's mind was also elsewhere. Her dinner with the commander troubled her greatly but for the life of her she couldn't work out quite why. She was resolved to be a perfectly horrid yet polite dinner guest.

Maps, finally coming to his senses, explained that they would be tired after flying anyway, so as disappointing as the cancellation was, it wasn't the end of the world and another time will have to be arranged.

Then just as Chipper approached with cups of hot tea, Maps leaned over and gently gave Victoria what he hoped would be a reassuring kiss on the cheek.

"What on earth are you doing?" shrieked Victoria.

"Well, I thought ..." stammered Maps.

"Well, don't think," scolded Victoria. Then as she looked up at Chipper, she thanked him, whilst Maps moved from her chair to the window and crumbled in embarrassment.

"I'm not used to being pecked by people," she explained. "If I had wished to be pecked, I would have visited an aviary!"

"Besides, this morning has been very hectic. I have received three proposals of undying love, an offer, if that's how you would describe it, of dinner with the commander and one highly offensive wolf whistle from the driver of a delivery wagon. I'm in no mood to be pecked."

Victoria had quite enough advanced behaviour for one day. Maps apologised and asked for some forgiveness. Victoria offered to forgive on the sound understanding that he wouldn't do anything of that sort again. Maps reluctantly agreed. Chipper chuckled quietly into his teacup.

The three of them drank their tea before Victoria excused herself and left.

"Well, that went well!" Chipper offered Maps his opinion.

Maps grumbled a response, whilst making his way to the map cupboard where he withdrew another map of the local area. Spreading the map open on the chart table in the centre of the room, he called Chipper over to discuss a route for the afternoon.

After climbing out of the airfield, they would turn northeast and head out towards the local town, easily recognisable due to its distinctive church. After passing over the town they agreed to follow the coastline in a northerly direction until they reached the mouth of the river estuary, whereupon they would head back toward the airfield landing in time for a late dinner. The route agreed, Maps and Chipper decided to head out to the aeroplane to see if it was fit to fly.

The Hangar Floor

Big Freddie and his mate Sparky were attending to the machine that Maps and Chipper would maybe fly later that day. Both were highly skilled, intelligent yet underutilized. They could fix aeroplanes with ease. They were both riggers and mechanics, and both had trained hard to get where they were, yet for all their efforts the pilots seemed to get great pleasure from breaking the aeroplanes. Both enjoyed their work, but both were of the opinion that the job was pretty thankless.

Freddie was cursing and swearing as he hauled on a crowbar that was attached to the wheel axle of the aeroplane. Sparky was sitting behind a worktable examining the dismantled parts of a magneto that he had carelessly strewn across the bench. Under any normal pressure he would have placed the parts neatly and in a good order. Today, however, he had seen so many magnetos that his hands were sore and his mind firmly elsewhere.

Freddie took a short break from his straining long enough to wipe the grease on his hands down the sides of his trousers. Sparky turned to his work mate, inadvertently knocking a vital piece of the magneto to the floor. He cursed his luck and set about looking for the part.

"Did you find it?" Freddie asked.

Sparky looked up at his mate and nodded.

"I have it," he said. "Plus, I found a couple of sixpence pieces down there."

Maybe Sparky's luck had changed.

Maps and Chipper arrived at the hangar to find the normally bustling hangar strangely deserted. They introduced themselves to the workmen, who in turn introduced themselves.

"Is there an aeroplane available?" enquired Maps.

Freddie looked around at the collection of aeroplanes assembled within the hangar. There was one in the corner with no engine. "We borrowed that engine for the aeroplane that crashed last week," he explained.

In the other corner of the hangar was a substantially complete aeroplane.

"Is that one available?" asked Maps.

Freddie escorted Maps to the aeroplane. All appeared in order. There was an engine, and all the wings were attached and appeared to have been correctly rigged. From its polished cowling to the tip of its elaborate tail, this aircraft promised much. Maps caressed the cowling, Freddie assured him that the engine was as clean as a whistle, Maps took his word for it before examining the large propeller, the edges of which bore no nicks or holes the surface was beautifully smooth and polished. Rounding the far wingtip maps he plucked one of the rigging wires, which gave off a satisfying sound. He admired the crisp fabric that covered the wings. On peering into the cockpit, however, he was amazed to find a large hole in the fabric where there should have been a seat.

"There is no seat!" Maps noted aloud.

Freddie popped his head in the cockpit and had to agree with Maps. Indeed there was no seat and no fabric where it should have been.

"We had to borrow that seat to use as a card table last night," Freddie explained.

Apparently in the heat of the moment, some of the other mechanics had stolen their card table to use as kindling for a fire. The fabric underneath it was used as an oily rag to start the fire.

"It all looks a bit dire in here. Do you think you can have an aeroplane ready for this evening?" Maps asked.

Freddie scratched his head. There was a wheel he could take off one, if only he could remove the wheel from the one he was working on. Sparky would have to find all the pieces for his magneto and fit it to the engine. Thankfully, the rigging appeared all in order and there was a seat somewhere in the hangar that he could use.

"It will be tough, but I reckon we could manage one aeroplane," Freddie concluded.

Maps thanked him and promised the two mechanics an amount of beer if the job was done. Freddie thanked Maps and he and Sparky got back to work.

Just as the conversation finished, the light from outside the hangar dimmed slightly. Freddie and Sparky leapt to their feet leaving Maps and Chipper slightly bemused. Chipper mocked the two mechanics who didn't flinch in response.

"You two," barked the commander, "come here!"

As Maps and Chipper turned towards the commander standing at the door, the colour from Chipper's face drained as he walked toward him. Freddie and Sparky also began to walk forward, then Freddie tripped on Maps's shoes and a muffled expletive was heard.

"Not you two!" the commander barked once more.

All four stopped walking instantly. It was only then that the commander pointed at Maps and Chipper. Freddie and Sparky stood firm until the commander gestured at them.

"Is that aeroplane fit to fly?" the commander shouted.

"It's as good as new," Sparky replied.

"It's good enough for students," Freddie stated.

"Which is it, gentlemen?" he asked, irritated. "Is the aeroplane as good as new or just good enough for a couple of students?"

Sparky was surprised by the commander's comments. He explained that it was normal for students to approach them asking for faults to be built into the repairs. Students, on the whole, didn't actually like flying. Freddie concurred wholeheartedly with Sparky, adding that this attitude was particularly prevalent amongst students flying without instructors.

"Naturally," Freddie concluded. "We thought you would be pleased that the aeroplane was in pieces."

"Pleased!" the commander screamed. "These two have a vitally important job to do later today, and I would rather hope that their aeroplane would be in a flyable condition to do the job."

The commander stared at Maps hoping he would add his authority to the rather one-sided conversation. Maps took the hint and proceeded to stomp around the hangar pointing at various components of aeroplanes and commenting on the state of the components. Faux authority had never sat comfortably with Maps; he reckoned that he was simply not that sort of chap. On this occasion, however, if it pleased the commander it was a means to an end.

Maps continued to berate the workmen, who listened aware of the rather comical grilling he was giving them, whilst smirking and giggling to themselves. Once Maps finished, he and Chipper turned and left the hangar and the workmen in peace.

Sparky looked at Freddie, and both shrugged their shoulders and simultaneously muttered "Students!"

As Maps and Chipper walked the short distance back to the flight planning room, Chipper's curiosity got the better of him.

"Why do students not want to fly?" he asked. "It seems like madness!"

Maps agreed that it was madness but explained that many students lacked courage and the confidence to be in the air without the insurance of an instructor. Many felt scared as the air currents tossed the aeroplane about.

"Your ability to remain cool and in control under those circumstances is what makes you such a good pilot." he explained to Chipper.

Chipper smiled to himself. He had never been placed in the high esteem by a colleague and called "a good pilot" before.

"Your ability under arduous conditions and your willingness to fly is what makes us such a good team," Maps continued.

Chipper nodded his agreement.

"Why then, did you shout at the mechanics?" Chipper enquired.

Maps explained that the shouting was all part of the game, a game that flyers and mechanics played.

"What game is that?" Chipper queried.

"The usual military game," Maps replied. "You remember that we talked about the game before. Well, this is all part of the game. We, the pilots, shout at the mechanics, the mechanics call us all the names under the sun, and eventually an aeroplane fit to fly appears and we all share a beer or two together."

Chipper didn't really understand the rules of the game. He found it all very impolite.

"Wouldn't it be easier to simply ask them nicely?" he asked.

"Ask?" replied Maps. "If we ask nicely, they will carry on as if nothing had happened and then nobody would fly."

Chipper still found it difficult to understand but consoled himself with the thought that it was only a game, and he would eventually understand the whys and wherefores."

Maps calmed Chipper by adding that they would go back in an hour or two and all would be well with the machine.

"They are very professional people after all," he explained. "They may grumble a little from time to time, but they take immense pride in producing an aeroplane. Now let's go and have a good cup of tea."

"Another one?" Chipper questioned, before they both headed for the nearest kettle.

Secret Wood

Years at universities around the country had taught the engineers, scientists and technicians well. Each had earned a place at the secret factory in the Secret Wood, and most if not all were very content with their lot. Obviously, the remote location and the lack of life-defining relationships were drawbacks, but they were doing the work they had trained for. Not one, however, could understand why as soon as they put a white coat on, they were called a boffin!

The crash of the first prototype was seen as a setback, but the second was already complete and ready to fly. Under any normal situation the crash of prototype 1 would be thoroughly investigated and any necessary corrective actions would be built into prototype 2. These were, however, far from normal times. The government had been particularly generous in their allocation of funds to the aircraft factories and most of the money had been spent. Two large aircraft had been produced and one had even flown, if only briefly. Progress being made could be demonstrated. The senior boffins were, by and large, confident that their work was valued and would be continued. The boffins were proud of their achievement in building the world's biggest aeroplane. All they had to do now was show that the aeroplane would fly and that it could be relied upon to fly.

Today was a big day, however, the day that the second prototype of the aeroplane they had worked so hard to build would soon be heading skyward. The atmosphere was tense and excited when the memo announcing a meeting was circulated. Piling into the large hangar each boffin waited with bated breath to hear what the boss was to say.

The boss cleared his throat, strode as authoritatively as he could to podium, and cleared his throat once more before he announced to the assembled technical team that the first flight of the second aeroplane was to be made today. The aeroplane was ready and the two pilots for the day were to be Arthur "Chilly" Chilton and Bill Masters. The purpose of the flight was to investigate the handling qualities of the aeroplane.

Chilly Chilton, as he was widely known, was to be the primary pilot on the flight; he was a seasoned flyer with many hours under his belt. He was a very technical chap, having studied engineering at university. Chilly had learnt to fly in the very early days of flight and had risen to the exalted rank of Chief Test Pilot with the company mainly due to his ability and calmness in the air. Indeed, he had only crashed two airplanes in ten years of flying.

Bill Masters on the other hand was simply a good enough pilot, with little understanding of the mechanics of flight. He was, however, the son of the owner of the local tyre manufacturer and therefore vital to the boffins, as the aeroplanes tyres could be purchased at a lower price than was normal. He was also notable for the lack of a suitable nickname although the thought of Chilly and Billy flying together often amused some people.

The sound of chatter rose in the room as each of the boffins knew that if the aeroplane could get through this test, the ministry would be on the verge of ordering it into production. As the chatter died down, the door to the meeting room opened and in walked Stevens, the man from the ministry. He walked to the front of the room and addressed the group. Stevens wasn't a good orator, and aware of this shortcoming, he kept things brief and simple. Emphasising that today was a big day, and the government hoped that all would go well, he told the meeting that on completion of the flight and a few other minor tests that the boffins need not worry about, the government would be pleased to help financially with the building of the first production batch.

His words were met with a large cheer, and it was with a big smile that the boss led Stevens into the adjoining hangar to partake of a small beverage and to view the, now complete, second prototype. The boss explained that following tests of the first aeroplane, the second one was sitting outside ready to be flown. The crash of the first prototype was simply down to bad luck and only to be expected when designing aeroplanes this advanced. Stevens agreed that the crash was unfortunate, he was also keen to learn about how the second aeroplane had been built without prior knowledge of the weaknesses of the first. The boss explained that some of the weaknesses had already been known and that the flight had been taken with risk, but that the boffins had done a magnificent job redesigning various features, in the light of the prototype 1's weaknesses.

"Such as?" inquired Stevens.

The boss began to list the modifications, explaining that the cockpit had been far too small and as a consequence been widened. Both sets of wings had to be redesigned to accept the greater weight of the more powerful engines needed to fulfill the requirement. The undercarriage also had to be strengthened and for the same reason. The tail had to be reprofiled to allow a better angle on take-off. The tail wheel had become a nose wheel and as such the wings had to be given a new angle.

"It's all pretty simple stuff really," the boffin said casually justifying the long list.

Stevens suggested that all that work must have cost the government a fortune, but the boffin eased his alarms by stating that the aeroplane would shorten the war considerably. The faintest hint of a smile crossed Stevens's face, suggesting that such a dismissive attitude wasn't what he was expecting, before asking what had been done to save government money.

The boss hadn't anticipated such an awkward question from his paymasters, but he began to list the items deleted from the design. Most of the protection for the pilot and occupants had been removed; the pesky flaps had also been removed.

"Flaps?" questioned Stevens.

"Yes, flaps. They are devices that help the aircraft take off and land in smaller spaces," the boss replied.

"So it takes longer to take off?" Stevens asked.

The boss agreed, but to mitigate this minor inconvenience the airfield manager lengthened the runway in the Secret Wood.

"Lengthened? By how much?" Stevens asked.

"Only a mile or so," the boss replied.

"A mile!" screeched Stevens.

"Or so," replied the boss. "It's a different budget, however."

After much to-ing and fro-ing Stevens, managed to extract the exact distance from the boffin.

"Two miles!" he screeched once more. "How much did that cost?"

As it was a different budget, the boss would never know the real cost; however, he imagined that cost would be more than recouped through the benefits to the project. The cost of the requisition of the wooded land, the cutting down of trees and then the levelling of the ground, and so on, and so on, the boss imagined would never be known. Stevens grumbled a little as he imagined the financial landscape the project had carved from the budgets.

Soon the boss, tiring of this administrative nonsense, ushered Stevens outside to show him the aeroplane. The huge biplane gleamed majestically in the bright sunshine, its eight engines shattering the silence as the two men stood and looked at the magnificent machine. Its silver painted finish reflected the sun's rays; it looked quite magnificent, very modern looking and incredibly large. The noise from the engines, however, was quite uncomfortable to listen to.

"The noise isn't so bad here. You should hear what it is like inside the aeroplane," the boss shouted. "The pilots have to fill their ears with cotton wool and use an extra thick leather helmet when flying." Stevens could only imagine what the pilots were hearing, as his getting any closer to the aeroplane proved to be painful.

Sitting in the cockpit, Chilly and Billy ran through the many preflight checks and when all was deemed correct they advanced the throttles. The noise suddenly became quite unbearable and so Stevens and the boffin retired to the relative quiet of the newly constructed observation tower, from where they could watch the aeroplane take off on its test flight.

The aircraft made its slow and steady progress to the farthest reaches of the wood. A quick glance at the windsock confirmed that a tight turn was required to line the aeroplane up into the wind. Chilton advanced the downwind engines and turned the aeroplane carefully into correct alignment.

Chilly Chilton tightened his seat belt and satisfied himself that all was well before he eased the throttles forward a little more and the aeroplane began to move. Inside the observation tower, the boss thought it a good idea to put the kettle on and make a cup of tea for the minister.

After confirming that the aeroplane was indeed into the wind, the pilot pushed the throttles all the way forward and with a cacophony of sound that sent birds flying from the trees for miles around, the aeroplane slowly began to accelerate.

Stevens sipped at his hot tea as the aeroplane slowly gathered speed. The noise from the engines increased as the aeroplane bounced along the grass runway. As it drew level with the tower, it began to bounce and jump over the bumps in the turf. Eventually the pilot eased back on his control stick and the aeroplane crawled majestically into the air, climbing ever so slowly towards the trees at the far end of the field. Inside the cockpit, the copilot began hauling as hard as he could on a string that would pull the wheels into housings on the side of the fuselage and nose. This process took almost a minute of hard pulling to accomplish, but eventually the two pilots heard a clunk as the doors shut enclosing the wheels. The copilot tied the string to the peg on the side of the cockpit and tried to relax.

"Gear up!" he shouted.

Stevens, however, found it difficult to relax; he had just seen the pride and joy of the government scientific program take a mile and a half to get into the air. "What happens when we put soldiers and all of their equipment into the aeroplane?" he asked.

"Naturally with such a weight on board the aeroplane takes a small but hardly noticeable performance hit, but we have thought of that," replied the boss with a smile.

"Well, what have you thought?" the minister persisted.

"Well, in order to shorten the take-off run, we are going to strap rockets to the fuselage to give it a bit of a boost," the boss announced.

"Why were they not used today?" the minister persisted.

The boffin explained that the first time they had used rockets, the rockets had set fire to the tail of the aeroplane and the flight had to be abandoned.

"Fire?" the minster asked.

The boffin reiterated that rockets were his preferred solution; however, since the fire, the team was working on a bungee assisted take-off system. Stevens expressed surprise that a bungee would work but asked to be present when it was tested.

"The bungee is a sure-fire winner," explained the boss. "But it does need quite a lot of manpower."

"Quite a lot?" the minister queried.

"Well yes, about 100 to 150," the boffin clarified.

"My, that is an awful lot of men," the minister noted.

The two pilots continued to climb heading east towards the sea, where they would perform a gentle turn through 180 degrees, followed by a few stalls and vertical maneuvers before heading back to the Secret Wood. Both pilots hoped and prayed that it would be a routine and easy trip. Now that they were airborne neither pilot had much choice.

After fifteen minutes the aeroplane had climbed to a respectable height. Throttling back the engines allowed the pilots to overfly the local town without causing too much disturbance to the residents.

"We are a lot higher than the last flight," Masters informed his pilot.

Leaning over he tapped Chilton on the arm pointed in the direction of the new heading – northeast. Chilton nodded his approval before turning the aircraft and heading for the coast.

The short distance to the coast was covered quickly as the aeroplane was pulled along by the enormous propellers and powerful engines. Masters and Chilton both had an opportunity to cast their eyes about over the patchwork earth that raced beneath them.

Flying

"Contact!" shouted Chipper.

The ground crew gave the propeller a mighty pull and with a puff of smoke the engine started. Chipper set the throttle to allow the engine to warm, settling back in his seat to think about the takeoff. Maps sat a bit uneasily in his seat. Despite the hours the two spent flying each other around, Maps was still not all together comfortable with someone else at the controls.

The mechanics had done a fine job getting the aeroplane ready. The engine roared away ahead of them, settling Maps's apprehension. The seats were far from comfortable, but the two men were accustomed to a little discomfort and neither thought much of the inconvenience.

After a moment or two to consult his maps and start his stopwatch, Maps instructed Chipper to fly slightly right of north to pick up the coast whereupon he should follow the coastline north. Chipper nodded his agreement and turned the aeroplane into the wind. With a gentle pressure on the throttle the aeroplane picked up speed, bounced lightly over the grass and gracefully eased itself into the air. Once the aircraft had climbed for a moment or two, Chipper swung the nose about and set a northeasterly course.

The aircraft settled into a gentle climb to altitude. There were few clouds about, and this afforded both men a wonderfully unobstructed view of the terrain below them. Climbing ever higher over the local town, with its distinctive church, Maps pointed out the coast a long way below them, Chipper nodded once more and maneuvered the aeroplane until he was accurately following the coastline. Maps carefully photographed the landmarks as the aeroplane sailed over them.

With the flight proceeding normally, Chipper could relax a little as a strong tail wind assisted the little biplane in its northerly direction. The cold of the altitude was making Chipper feel a little uncomfortable, pulling at the collar of his flying coat and ducking low behind the windscreen as he tried to keep himself warm. Maps, in the rear of the aeroplane, didn't have the benefit of a large windscreen; and despite the layers of warm clothing he had on, he was also beginning to feel the cold. They continued to fly along in total silence, each believing that the other was having a wonderful time.

After approximately one and three-quarter hours, Maps noticed something to the left of the aeroplane. A small flash of light caught his attention. He leaned forward and tapped Chipper on the shoulder and pointed in the direction of the light. Both strained their eyes in the direction of the light. Maps decided that a closer inspection of this object would firstly afford them a flight at a lower and warmer altitude, and secondly give them something to do. He leaned forward and once again tapped Chipper on the shoulder. Having grabbed Chipper's attention, he began to point in the direction he wanted Chipper to fly. Chipper acknowledged Maps with a nod of his head and hauled the nose of the aeroplane over to the left.

In the cockpit of the secret aeroplane, all was not well. Approximately half an hour earlier whilst cruising over the waters of the wash, the two pilots engaged the secret aeroplane in a series of high banked turns and dives. During the course of a particularly energetic turn, both heard a crack and a twang coming from one of the wings. The pilot immediately asked Masters to get into the back of the aeroplane and have a look at what the trouble was. Whilst Masters was away from his seat, Chilton began to observe the oil pressure falling in one of the engines. He immediately decided to shut down the errant engine. No sooner had the propeller on the engine stopped turning than Masters returned with very bad news.

"The engine has come away from its mountings!" he screamed, making sure that Chilton had heard him.

Chilton knew the aeroplane intimately and was aware of the consequences of the malfunction. Masters assured him that no fire had been seen; however, Chilton wasn't so sure and asked Masters to check. Loosening his belts, Masters looked through the window behind him. A fire had now started; the loose engine had ruptured its fuel line, which was now pouring fuel onto the hot exhausts. Alarmed at the prospect of fire in a wood and fabric aeroplane, Chilton began a search for somewhere to land but he was miles from anywhere familiar. To crash land an aeroplane as big and as fast as this was sure to be a suicidal adventure.

Chipper remained high and to the rear of the big aeroplane, but still the speed of the secret aeroplane prevented Chipper from coming alongside it. Soon they both saw that the whole wing appeared to be covered in smoke, and then appeared to be on fire. The loss of an engine caused the big secret aeroplane to slow. Chipper noticed that the aeroplane was slowing and took his opportunity to dive his own aeroplane in order to come alongside the malfunctioning one.

Maps was as cool and professional as ever, keeping a close eye on the position of the aeroplane, allowing himself a moment or two, now and again, to check the markings on the big aeroplane. After all it might not be one of theirs.

As Chipper skillfully brought his aeroplane alongside, he made as many notes about it as he could. He noted that it was an aeroplane with large British symbols on the side; he further noted that it was an amazingly fast aeroplane! Peering into the cockpit area, Chipper noted movement. Maps was also incredibly impressed by the aeroplane. He laid down his maps and, using his notebook, he began to jot down notes in case he should be asked to recall details of the encounter later. He noted that it was big, very fast, and on fire! The smoke trailing behind the aeroplane was thick and acrid. The pilots in an enclosed cabin looked terrified! The fire was coming from one of the four engines and was beginning to burn through the fabric of the wings. Things, it would appear, weren't going well on the aeroplane.

Chipper pushed the throttle as far forward as it would go as he tried to get every last little bit of power from his single engine aeroplane. Maintaining his position alongside the fast aeroplane he signalled to the crew. Chipper offered a thumbs-up sign to his fellow pilot, a gesture that he would later reflect was probably not at all appropriate. The pilot in the enclosed cockpit gave him a thumbs-down sign, and a sign that Chipper felt later was entirely appropriate.

Chipper decided that the only thing to do was to help them look for an airfield. Maps was a step ahead of his pilot and already plotted a course to an airfield in a wood, a place called Secret Wood.

Chipper took the new course and, beckoning the pilot of the fast burning aeroplane to follow him, he set off. Soon the distinctive church in the local town came into view. *Almost there*, Chipper thought. Maps pointed Chipper in the correct direction to the Secret Wood and with a tap on the shoulder and a point in the correct direction, the aeroplane was turned, the secret aeroplane following closely behind.

Stevens and the boss were still in the tower when the two aeroplanes came into view. Stevens was the first to notice the trail of smoke. The boffin desperately tried to excuse the smoke, explaining that it was a normal consequence of the type of oil they were using. Sadly, as the smoke-trailing aeroplane got closer, it became more and more difficult for the boss to hide the fact that the secret aeroplane was on fire.

As Maps and Chipper's little training biplane screamed low over the top of the tower, Chipper was straining at the controls in an attempt to prevent them crashing into the woods. Maps looked behind to watch what he thought would undoubtedly be a calamitous crash landing.

The secret aeroplane made the field just in time, the fuselage bouncing off the tops of the trees short of the runway. There was no time for the pilots to release the undercarriage, and consequently, the aeroplane belly flopped onto the turf of the airfield and began to slide, turning as it did towards the tower. Stevens and the boffin stood with saucer-sized eyes as the out-of-control aeroplane slid towards them. With an almighty crash the wing gave way, sending the loose engine cartwheeling into the woods where it started an alarmingly large fire. With a crack, the last embers of what once was a wing gave way, sending the wing cartwheeling after the engine into the wood.

It took a few seconds before Stevens and the boss felt safe enough to pick themselves up from the floor and peer through the window. Outside a line of boffins were hurriedly organising a line along that they would pass buckets of water to douse the fire. The wing lay smoldering in the ditch that separated wood from the airfield. In front of the observation tower, the large aeroplane lay shattered on the grass. The cockpit had separated from the fuselage and was lying on its side. The tail surfaces had also come adrift and were lying on the grass many metres ahead of the cockpit. Fortunately, the pilots all appeared safe. Emerging slowly from the wreckage, they looked up and waved at the circling Maps and Chipper. Maps tapped Chipper on the shoulder, and they set course for home.

Dinner

In her quarters Victoria dressed in a manner that she hoped wouldn't encourage the commander. She chose a very professional outfit with a long skirt that covered her ankles and almost her shoes. A newly starched white blouse seemed appropriate for the occasion, but she chose not to use makeup or to do anything special with her hair. After dressing, Victoria spent a short time going over her topics for conversation. Finding most of them rather dull, she decided that her best tactic was not to decide. She resolved, however, not to allow the commander any opportunity to flirt or be overly friendly.

A car arrived and whisked her off to a local restaurant, a distance from the camp that wasn't too far but far enough to prevent anyone seeing them. A smartly dressed waiter welcomed Victoria offering her a glass of champagne, which she declined in favour of a glass of water. Experience told her that champagne often made her as silly as a sausage!

In a dimly lit corner of the restaurant, sat the commander, his face lit by the candles on the table, yet partially hidden by a bunch of fine roses. Victoria stopped in her tracks upon seeing this arrangement; it looked for all the world as if he were here to seduce and not to entertain. On seeing Victoria, the commander smiled, rose from his seat and offered her the other seat at the table. He was smart and courteous and obviously had other things on his mind. Victoria needed to take his mind off those other things.

"How is your wife this evening?" she asked.

The commander almost choked on his drink, wondering how on earth she knew he was married.

"Your wedding ring, sir," she remarked, pointing to the commander's finger where a prominent wedding ring sat.

"She is fine and is sorry that she couldn't join us this evening," the commander lied.

Victoria engaged the commander in several minutes of conversation about his wife. It appeared that she had come down with a cold. The commander left her at home to look after the children they reared.

"If you like I can pop round with a remedy from the pharmacy," Victoria suggested.

"My wife isn't one for a fuss," he replied, suggesting a visit wasn't necessary.

Still, Victoria persisted, determined to make the commander feel as uneasy as she could.

The commander looked for any way out of the conversation, but Victoria, like a terrier after a rabbit, would just not let go. Eventually the commander managed to distract with the mention of Maps and Chipper.

"That Chipper is a damned good pilot," he announced as the first course arrived.

Victoria took the bait, much to the commander's relief, but still she was proving to be a decidedly difficult dinner guest.

"Perhaps he could hear that from you," she replied.

The commander offered the opinion that it would be much more meaningful if he heard it secondhand from her. Victoria understood the plan, however; the commander wanted Maps and Chipper to know that he had dinner with Victoria.

"I will send him around to your office tomorrow morning, if that's okay?" she told the commander.

Reluctantly the commander had to back down and offered to see Chipper in the very near future.

Victoria tucked into a fine meal, making sure to tell the commander how grateful she was for the dinner. As the evening finally drew to a close, the commander paid an enormous bill and the two walked slowly to the exit.

The commander summoned his car and thanked Victoria for her company.

"I do hope we can do this again sometime soon," he told her.

"I do hope your wife gets better soon, and maybe she could join us," Victoria replied. "Wouldn't that be nice?"

"Indeed," the commander lied once more.

The car drove Victoria back to her quarters at the hospital and the commander back to his house.

The Man in the Surf

After a week or so deciphering messages and chatting to contacts, Arnold needed to get down to the beach once more. He had heard on his grapevine that someone or something would be there for him.

The bus ride from the town to the beach was uncomfortable and interminably long. Finally, after what seemed like ages, the sea came into view. After stepping off the bus, Arnold made his way down to the sea front. He consulted a small map he was given and set off, uncertain of what would await him.

The walk to the allotted spot took Arnold along the promenade where he happened upon a lone fisherman selling local crab in sandwiches. Arnold bought a sandwich and walked down to the shoreline eating merrily. He calculated that the allotted spot was at least a mile away, and as he set off in the right direction he tried to look as inconspicuous as possible. His long overcoat covered most of his Wellington boots and this protected him from the sea and the slight drizzle that was falling. Rounding the bottom of a sizeable cliff, Arnold spotted what he had come here for: a round metallic object bobbing around in the waves.

Wading out into the surf, Arnold found that the water was a little deeper than he had imagined. Water poured into his Wellingtons giving him cause to pause. The task of retrieving the metallic object was, however, of the utmost importance to him, so he continued. The water reached waist-level when Arnold could finally grab the metallic object. Cradling the object tightly in his arms, Arnold returned to shallower waters and the beach.

Victoria had earned a day off and she too had made her way to the beach. She loved the sound of the ocean and the fresh air that abounded at the sea front. The rock pools took her back to a more carefree time when she could happily play for hours amongst them.

It was always the seaside that Victoria would use to clear her head, generally relax and let go. She found herself walking near the cliffs when she observed a man waist-deep in water appearing to retrieve something from the surf.

In normal times Victoria would simply have ignored the rather odd happenstance, but these were no ordinary times. She looked around hoping that there was a gentleman available to assist her, but sadly there were none. So, she took it upon herself to question the man in the surf.

"Ahoy there!" she yelled to the man. Asking if the man needed any help offered her time to come up with a plan.

The man stepped from the surf and tried to scuttle away as if he cared little for the lady on the shore.

"Did you catch anything nice?" Victoria yelled at the man.

Arnold stopped in his tracks and turned to look at the young lady. "Catch?" he questioned.

Victoria pushed the point whilst trying to be as polite as she could. Arnold explained that he had a lobster pot and was hurrying home to cook the lobster.

"I didn't know there were lobsters in there. Can I see it?"

Arnold paused; he was deeply in a pickle now. He explained that he had no permission to take lobsters from the sea and was in a hurry to get away as quickly as he could. Arnold then explained that he wouldn't want to get Victoria into any trouble. "So, if you don't mind …," he concluded.

Victoria explained that she was hungry – she only ate variations on rabbit stew at the flying school. Arnold's interest in the lady piqued when she mentioned the flying school. He explained that there was a genuinely nice crab sandwich to be had on the promenade.

"Would you like one?" Arnold inquired.

Victoria had to admit to herself that she was indeed hungry. She had also heard that the local crab was very tasty. She also was becoming more and more interested in the object the man had hidden under his coat. She accepted the offer and introduced herself to the man. Arnold gave his name in return and the two set off toward the promenade.

A little while later, the two sat on the sea wall tucking into their crab sandwiches whilst Arnold tried to disguise the object and extract as much information from Victoria as he could.

Victoria gave him as little information as she could. She felt it wise not to talk too freely. However, as an hour or so passed Victoria began to enjoy the company of this strange yet interesting man.

Arnold sensed that the conversation was turning away from the flying school, its location and the equipment located there. He also desperately needed an excuse to leave the young lady.

"I really must dash. I have a bus to catch," he explained. The water that inundated his clothes was making him very cold by now.

"I could walk with you," Victoria offered, but Arnold hastily declined.

Before Victoria could stall him anymore, Arnold strode off into the distance, squelching as he went, and melted into the background.

It was early evening when Arnold arrived back at his accommodation. Stepping through his front door and closing it, he was finally able to remove the object from under his coat. He placed the object on the table in the kitchen and examined it more closely. Finding a screwdriver in the drawer under the table, he began to carefully dismantle it.

Inside the object was a series of papers that Arnold would study long into the night.

Opposition

High on a hill overlooking a splendidly beautiful wooded plain, sat a beautiful white castle, its towers affording the occupants a commanding view of the wonderful countryside. The people who lived and worked in the castle were aware of how lucky they were. The food was prepared by an excellent chef, and the cellar was brim full of beers and wines. All agreed that this was a simply marvellous place to be.

Since hostilities had broken out, however, the castle had been turned over to the country's aeronautical elite. Commanded by a tall, handsome and inspirational leader known as the Baron Bardufloss, the castle and its adjoining aerodrome was a happy, yet a ruthlessly efficient place to develop aerial strategies and to practice aerial warfare. Bardufloss loved the order of the place and worked hard keeping his flyers at the peak of efficiency.

On the afternoon train from the capital, seventeen top brass generals and marshals prepared for a meeting with Bardufloss. They hoped that their notepads would soon be full of secretive plans. They also hoped that their bellies would soon be full of fine wines, beers, and well-prepared food.

News from the front wasn't good, and something simply had to be done. A daring mission was in the offing, and with the risks and dangers of this mission, only one man could pull it off. The assembled top brass all agreed that a couple of days being entertained in the castle were well worth the time and effort of getting there.

The trip was an interminably long one, however. Being members of the military elite, they could rely on a little wine to keep them comfortable. Safely locked in a compartment, the head of the entourage produced a piece of paper that would enlighten the group to the nature of the visit.

"It appears that our man in England has observed a new type of flying machine," he started. "His information comes from the most reliable of sources: a greengrocer in the local town and an informant who has observed a number of special tyres being made at the local factory." He continued explaining there was only one team in the country that could destroy this new machine.

"Bardufloss's lot, I presume," a marshal remarked.

"Indeed!" the leader replied.

Bardufloss had been handpicked to lead an experimental division of the armed forces when war was declared. His ideas and notions underpinned most early thought on the prosecution of the war in the air. His "never say never" approach to flying was greatly admired amongst the higher echelons of the government. He was, indeed, in every sense a very highflyer. The only reservation that the leader had was that the team had never been put in harm's way. The leaders felt that Bardufloss would be raring to go, but the other members of his team might need some persuasion. They had been living the highlife in the castle and may not be prepared to risk that life for a mission that would stretch both man and machine to the limit.

The excitement in the compartment, and the wine, ensured that the journey continued with little fuss. Soon enough, as the mountains came into view, the engine slowed to a crawl and pulled into the station. Rising from their seats and finding that the wine had perhaps been consumed with a little too much enthusiasm, the top brass bounced from wall to wall as they headed to the train door.

The generals and marshals were met at the station by a fleet of carriages that quickly whisked them out of the town, through the delightfully wooded approaches to the castle, which was gleaming in the late afternoon sun. Barduffloss and his best troops were assembled in the courtyard, all in best dress uniform to meet the guests, unaware of the nature of the visit. Barduffloss felt a good show was vital to his continuing existence in the comfort of the castle.

The generals and marshals having decamped from the carriages were politely but quickly ushered into the grand surroundings of the great dining hall. Its wooden beamed ceilings and panelled walls quickly impressed the group, and after a taste of even yet more wine the head of the entourage introduced the reason for the visit.

A dangerous mission was to be undertaken; the other side was developing an aeroplane that could change the face of the war. The country needed its top pilots to fly over there and destroy it before the aeroplane could be developed any more.

On hearing the reason, the pilots, navigators, and groundcrews gasped and applauded, as they were expected to do.

"It sounds easy enough," Barduffloss replied naively. Once again the pilots, navigators, and groundcrews gasped. The mood in the room had begun to change.

The generals and marshals all smiled at Barduffloss's attitude. This is what they wanted to hear.

"Is that all you want us to do?" Barduffloss asked. Barduffloss's team again mumbled that they thought the mission was more risky than their leader was letting on.

The generals and marshals grumbled a little. They had thought that the mission would be enough for Bardufloss's team.

"If you could bring some of the aeroplane back with you, that would be great. Maybe take a few photographs, get a few specifications … all the usual stuff," the head of the delegation retorted.

Bardufloss nodded his agreement; he was keen to get going and immediately issued an order for his pilots to assemble in the next room.

Bardufloss was to join them after discussing the generals' plans in private. The generals kept the details brief and to the point. They explained that an agent in England had seen and reported the details of this new machine. Bardufloss read the report quickly. Enthusiastically, he announced that he was looking forward to telling his team. The generals told him to get going; there was no time to lose.

"Okay then … let's go!" Bardufloss announced. He headed to the door confident that this would be his time, his moment to write his name into history.

Bardufloss could hear the chatter of the pilots in the next room, so he decided it was time to find a few volunteers. In his usual confident manner, he went to address his unit.

"At last gentlemen," Bardufloss announced, "our time to take flight has arrived. History beckons."

The team cheered unenthusiastically, shifting around nervously as they waited to be convinced that Bardufloss hadn't taken leave of his senses.

"We have the information we need!" Barduffloss announced. "We know what it is and where it is. We just need to attack it".

Once more the pilots all cheered but with little enthusiasm.

"The aeroplane is fast," he elaborated. "It is big and capable of transporting a small army anywhere in Europe quickly. It's not guarded and often sits out in the open. This should be an easy task for us."

Bardufloss concluded his briefing with a request for volunteers. The pilots all cheered, as they were expected to, and all volunteered, as they were expected to.

Bardufloss dismissed his pilots. They mumbled quietly to one another as they left the meeting, confused about the role they would be assuming and how it could possibly have any impact upon their comfortable existence in the castle. These pilots were used to free-flowing wine and easy patrols along the borders of the war. Mostly, they were content with their lot. The aeroplanes they flew were quite often available and were considered to be the best machines in Northern Europe at that time. Suddenly their leader, Baron Bardufloss, shattered their existence with talk of a crazy mission, deep into opposition territory to destroy a large aeroplane.

The entire unit went to bed knowing that their world had changed and nothing would ever be the same again. Each slept the sleep of uneasy men.

After spending an equally restless night reflecting, Bardufloss detected a hint of disinterest in his pilots as they all joined him for breakfast. Later that day, he called them together for a training flight. The generals and marshals expected that sort of thing, and Bardufloss was determined not to disappoint them.

In the days preceding the visit, Bardufloss had made sure that as many aeroplanes as possible would be available. Aeroplanes were fixed, engines were tuned and cleaned. Pilots' best uniforms were cleaned and pressed, and every spare moment was spent polishing shoes and belt buckles.

The generals and the marshals awoke to witness twenty-three brightly coloured biplanes all starting their engines in unison. One by one, and with split-second timing, they maneuvered to the take-off area. Bardufloss lead the formation, gesticulating wildly at his pilots, after a fashion he had turned the formation into the wind. Bardufloss's chest swelled with pride as he moved the throttle forward to its maximum position. The biplane shuddered slightly before picking up speed and becoming airborne. Bardufloss circled the airfield and waited for his colleagues to follow. Satisfied that everyone was in the correct position, Bardufloss led the formation behind the castle and out of sight.

The generals and marshals smiled at the efficiency and the teamwork on display for them. They retired into the castle and, after stopping for a sip or two of wine, climbed the stairs to the roof where they could get a better view.

A grin of satisfaction spread across Bardufloss's face as he looked left and right and saw the wonderful sight of his pilots all looking inward and maintaining immaculate position. All the hours of instruction and practice were paying off handsomely. All around him aeroplanes were bouncing on the air currents yet keeping perfect station with the lead aeroplane. Happy that all was well, Bardufloss eased the nose of his aeroplane above the prominent horizon and flew a perfect course toward the nearest clouds. The formation followed him as he enjoyed a few moments dancing his group along the tops of the clouds.

The generals and marshals watched from their vantage point on the roof as the noise from the formation subsided. They could now enjoy a little more of the castle's excellent hospitality in peace and quiet. After a glass or two of wine, the noise from the formation was heard once more. The gathering took a collective stride toward the edge of the roof to observe. On the ground in front of them, young men were staking a large white sheet to the ground. This would serve as a target for the group.

When Bardufloss saw the castle ahead of him, he gave a signal for the formation to descend and attack the target. Using guns and rockets, each pilot would follow the leader in a dive, attack the target and then ascend back to the leader's altitude. It was a simple enough manoeuvre, one that they had practiced time and again, and Bardufloss was confident that his team wouldn't let him down.

Pushing the stick forward and retarding the throttle, Bardufloss's aeroplane began to descend at an ever-increasing rate, its speed building up as the glide steepened. Bardufloss glanced behind him to see the rest of the formation following as they had been instructed to do. With precision and discipline, each of the twenty-three aeroplanes attacked the target. The generals and marshals delighted in the noise and the sight of a target being torn to shreds in front of them.

Bardufloss climbed after the attack and was soon joined by all of his pilots. The twenty-three strong formation flew a wide circuit of the castle before setting course for home, content with the job they just completed.

Arriving back at the castle, the formation streaked across the landing spot before executing a perfect climbing turn then circling to land.

Bardufloss welcomed each pilot home with a huge grin and a hearty shake of the hand. All twenty-three aeroplanes landed and were intact, Bardufloss was relieved to note. The generals and marshals descended from their lofty perch to congratulate Bardufloss and his men.

Once all of the aeroplanes were secured and moved to their hangarage, the generals, marshals, Bardufloss and all of his men retired to the dining room, where wine and fine food was waiting. The head of the delegation told Bardufloss that he thought the mission would be a piece of cake, and Bardufloss agreed. All were eager to start the planning and to get airborne as soon as possible.

Sights and Sounds

Chipper had been called into the commander's office early the next morning. Sadly, the commander's office was all too familiar to Chipper. He, on several occasions, had to stand and listen to the commander's decisions, decisions he felt were far too often made up on the spur of the moment. Still, here he was again, ready to accept whatever the commander felt was the correct course of action. Before entering the commanders' office, Chipper recognized that he was already resigned to his fate, but he was determined to give the commander a damned good listening to.

Chipper paused before entering the office. He made sure that he had on a clean and pressed uniform, as clean and as pressed as anyone who lived in a tent could be. His shoes gleamed under many layers of polish and his brasses equally gleamed in the morning sun. Chipper was as ready as he would ever be.

He strode forward and knocked as confidently as he could on the wooden door before taking a pace backward. The secretary opened the door and beckoned the young flyer into the office.

Beyond the internal door sat the commander, his head buried in paperwork. Occasionally, he could be heard muttering to himself. Chipper had a sense of foreboding not entirely unfamiliar to him. The secretary coughed politely and having grabbed the commander's attention she showed Chipper into his office.

On the desk in front of the commander was the beautifully crafted report he and Maps had submitted the previous day.

Unfortunately for Chipper, the content of the report kicked up quite a storm. The commander explained that Maps and Chipper's encounter with the secret aeroplane had left him with quite a dilemma. On the one hand, he should be commending the two of them for their actions in directing a stricken aeroplane to a place of safety. On the other hand, however, nobody should be aware of the secret aeroplane's existence. How could these two unqualified flyers be trusted with such sensitive information? The commander was also fresh from an ear-lashing that he received from Victoria and was determined to clip the wings of these two high-flying students.

He filled out the remainder of the form in front of Chipper and stamped it with a huge red stamp that read:

SECURITY RISK, CONFINED TO CAMP

Chipper left the office stunned and confused. Maps passed Chipper on his way to the commander's office, doubtless to be told the same thing. As they exchanged a few words, a young lad from the local village recognised them. The young lad was allowed on the station every day to deliver the newspapers and do general errands.

In his bag, the newspapers headlined breaking news. "Second Crash of the Secret Aeroplane" was splashed across the front page of one paper, and another headline read, "Secret Aeroplane Crashes … Again!" Most of the other papers had similar stories somewhere on their front page.

"Are you the two pilots that saw the secret aeroplane burst into flames and crash last night?" he asked the two friends.

"Yes, we are," replied a disheartened Chipper. "But for goodness sake, don't tell a soul about it."

"I won't," replied the young lad.

Maps entered the commander's office after a short pause whilst the commander read the freshly delivered newspaper. Maps marched smartly into the office, halted smartly and saluted the commander. On the desk was the report of the encounter, a report that was also splashed across the front pages.

The commander was, as always, a little mellower with Maps than he was with Chipper; after all Maps had already served his time at the front. The commander explained that it was Maps's duty to look after his younger and less experienced companion. The commander said that he felt disappointed with Maps's conduct in this operation. How could he allow such an inexperienced flyer anywhere near such a sensitive aeroplane?

"But it's secret, sir," answered Maps. "It's not like we went looking for it!"

Besides neither of them had the faintest idea that the aeroplane was secret. It wasn't like it had "SECRET" painted in large letters on its sides.

The commander politely asked Maps to keep his opinions to himself, and then reminded Maps of his duty to Chipper.

"Both you and he are in all probability going to be exceptional pilots," the commander explained. "It is, however, your duty to make sure that the young Chipper remains unhurt and is in a flying condition for as long as the two of you are billeted together."

The commander dismissed Maps after also confining him to camp until the storm over the secret aeroplane passed. How long that would be wasn't known, but the commander expected a great furor to erupt over the whole affair.

In the tent that Maps and Chipper occupied, the mood was a touch gloomy. Chipper removed his polished shoes and placed them carefully wrapped in a soft cloth at the bottom of his wardrobe, His uniform was carefully placed in the same wardrobe next to a line of clean shirts.

On the small table between the beds was a couple of tins of polish and a deck of cards. Both would come in very handy in the coming days. They were only confined to camp and not on report – no potato peeling, no parading about the school. The only real downside wasn't being able to meet friends and colleagues.

Both thought that things could have been so very much worse.

Sir Winston

The government was eagerly anticipating that aerial power would win the day; they were pouring hundreds of thousands of pounds into the industry. Production of aeroplanes was as high as it had ever been and even the training of pilots to fly these machines was increased on an almost daily basis. Whilst struggling to understand why all this expense was having such a limited impact on the continent, the ministry in charge of pilot training was summoned to appear before a government committee.

The meetings were widely reported in the press. Excuses abounded every day: the wrong type of fuel, the fragility of the machines, the complexity of the machines, the strength of the opposition – all reported by the media. Once the minister himself became tired of all the arguments, he summoned his under-secretary in charge of developing the military flying academies.

A few more days were expended whilst the minister and his under-secretary banded about ideas and suggestions, but all to no apparent avail. The under-secretary was convinced that the problem lay squarely at the door of the flying schools; they were simply not producing the sort of chap that the country needed. Therefore, logically it was the commanders of the schools who weren't commanding the respect of the students or instilling in those students the sort of courage and understanding that was required. So it was that the under-secretary for military pilot training decided to drop in on one of the schools that day.

The under-secretary, Sir Winston Winston-Frobisher, was the foremost expert on military pilot training. He learnt to fly before the war started and what he didn't know about flying was, frankly, not worth knowing. Within the government, he was a widely respected figure with the reputation for making sure that things got done. He wasn't a man to be trifled with.

The perceived failure of the training system was a matter of reputation for the Sir Winston and, as a man of high reputation, he found his name being associated with any type of failure intolerable. As the minister in charge, however, it was down to him alone to get to the bottom of the situation and sort it out. True to form, he spent several hours determining the cause and the solution to the problem. All that was left to do was to get his team on board.

It was getting late in the evening when he called his team together and briefed them all about his plan of action. He would visit several schools and give the commanders a piece of his mind. If actions weren't taken for sure heads would roll. He determined that an immediate start was necessary. The team of advisors and staffers knew what was best. All present congratulated Sir Winston on his brilliant plan and his decisive action.

So it was that plans were made, orders written and delivered, and accompanying staff informed. Keeping things to a minimum, Sir Winston nominated just himself and his secretary to the team that would travel to the various schools. The other team members would all be employed supporting the visits from the government offices they occupied.

Sir Winston's secretary arrived by train at the school, ahead of the knight who would naturally be flying into the school in his own aeroplane. Transferring to an automobile for the short journey to the school, the secretary reflected on the number of useful things she could have been doing had she been left back in the office.

The secretary was met by a very tired-looking commander who escorted him through the buildings that made up the school. The commander was sure that the secretary would just want to give the school the once over to make sure that everything Sir Winston would see was in order. The secretary assured the commander the visit was purely routine and that he would simply sign a piece of paper, say hello to a few people and soon be on his way.

The commander and the secretary spent the remainder of the morning in the commander's office attempting to get to the bottom of some of Sir Winston's more awkward questions. Sir Winston was extremely interested in accident rates, the academic qualifications of the students and aeroplane availability. The secretary and the commander were to have all the available information to hand by the time Sir Winston arrived.

The commander spent most of his lunchtime crunching numbers whilst Sir Winston's secretary busied herself pulling files from the cabinets positioned around the office. The secretary then came across Chipper's file, stamped "CONFINED TO CAMP."

"Is this the chap that saw the secret aeroplane?" she asked. The commander was surprised that the secretary knew about the secret aeroplane, but he nodded to confirm that Chipper was indeed the man she thought he was.

"How on earth do you know about the secret aeroplane?" he asked in an attempt to divert the secretary's focus.

The secretary explained that the aeroplane was common knowledge in the halls of government. "You cannot keep the finances of such a huge project secret for very long," she replied. The secretary then further explained that the minister in charge of the project was considered to be an eccentric chap who completely misunderstood the problems associated with the project.

Indeed, when the problems arose concerning the take-off distances that the aeroplane required, the minister simply built larger runways, ignoring the fact that his aeroplane also required an enormous area to be levelled before it could land anywhere. In the English shires this wasn't much of a problem – expensive but doable. What he minister failed to grasp was that to fulfill the purpose of the aeroplane, to deliver troops to the hotspots on the front lines, building an enormous runway close to the front would take time and be something of a giveaway for the opposition should they observe the runway's construction.

"I'm sure Sir Winston will want to see this man. Would that be at all possible?" the secretary returned to the question in hand.

The commander reluctantly agreed. He wasn't sure that a simple recruit should be singled out in this manner. The secretary assured the commander that the meeting would be very discrete; Sir Winston hated fuss. This information reassured the commander little because, in his experience, visits of this nature always included the maximum of fuss whilst achieving very little of any substance.

The commander called his secretary asked her to get Chipper prepared for the meeting with Sir Winston.

"Dress uniform?" she asked the commander.

"Dress uniform," he confirmed.

The secretary returned to her desk and began to call cleaners and polishers. When the commander said dress uniform, he meant what he said, so Chipper must look the part.

By mid-afternoon, the commander was getting a little fidgety. Sir Winston was overdue and the large majority of the school's work had halted in order to welcome the esteemed guest. The sound of an approaching aeroplane, however, calmed his nerves somewhat. Sir Winston flew an incredibly old-fashioned aeroplane; it was a large aeroplane of a parasol design. Sir Winston appeared to be suspended in a rather uncomfortable position beneath the aeroplane's single high-set wing, but the aeroplane appeared to be stable and under full control as it approached the airfield for a landing. Sir Winston skillfully landed his aeroplane and with a big kick of his rudder turned it towards the welcoming party.

As the propeller slowed to a stop, Sir Winston was greeted by the commander, who in turn offered his hand to Sir Winston. Sir Winston climbed from the aeroplane clambering over wheels and bracing wires. It was one of these wires that caught Sir Winston's foot offering the assembled crowd a first class view of the fall that twisted the knight's ankle. Sir Winston squealed as he turned his ankle, a squeal that a Knight of the Realm should really never be heard screaming. His protestations at the pain he suffered were also not the protestations a Knight of the Realm should be heard protesting.

The commander was as keen as ever to be seen by Sir Winston to be getting things done. He summoned two men from the nearby crowd to transport Sir Winston quickly as possible to the sick quarters. Sir Winston wasn't the most athletic of senior figures; his fondness for good brandy and large roast dinners had an adverse effect on his figure. In order to carry him to sick quarters, two more men and a large, wheeled cart were required. Even four men struggled to pick Sir Winston up. Complaining as loudly as he could, he was eventually transferred to cart and whisked away.

The commander tried to maintain a calm manner as Sir Winston was hurried along, however, his abiding concern at the time was that the delightful Victoria would not be on duty that day. The commander didn't want Sir Winston to hear of his dining arrangements with Victoria.

Sadly for the commander, Sir Winston was greeted at the door of the sick quarters by the wonderful Victoria. Sir Winston stopped squealing and protesting as his eyes fell upon her, his persona changing to a more heroic one, a persona much more befitting a Knight of the Realm.

Victoria quickly took charge and had Sir Winston quickly hurried off to see the doctor. On the way Victoria asked her patient his name.

"Winston Winston-Frobisher," he replied.

"Is that two Winstons or one?" Victoria enquired.

"Two, please," he replied. "It is actually Sir Winston Winston-Frobisher, but you may call me Sir."

Victoria was a little taken aback by his insistence on being called Sir, but she decided to play along anyway. She soon presented the knight in front of the doctor.

"This is Sir Winston Winston-Frobisher," she introduced. "He would like to be referred to as Sir." Then she added, "The poor little fellow had a small accident."

The doctor was a little perplexed by this insistence on the correct use of titles; after all it was the doctor who was holding the knife.

"I am Doctor James Rimmer," the doctor introduced himself. "You may call me Doctor."

Victoria and the doctor both smiled at the patient.

"Sir appears to have twisted an ankle," Victoria informed the doctor.

Doctor Rimmer approached Sir Winston and very carefully he examined the damaged ankle. He concluded that Sir Winston had sprained an ankle.

The doctor informed the patient that untwisting his ankle would take almost a week. A week in which Sir Winston mustn't under any circumstances put any weight on the ankle.

"Is that understood?"

This was bad news for Sir Winston; after all he had lots to do. Victoria quickly reassured the patient that she would do her utmost to make him as comfortable as possible. Sir Winston reflected on his stupidity yet was calmed by the presence of Victoria. He tried to imagine how life could be any worse. The affairs of state would, after all, have to be left alone for a week.

Maps and Chipper were busily playing cards when the Sir Winston and the cart passed close by their tent. Peeking outside Chipper remarked that maybe they should help out; however, Maps was less keen. His compassion subdued, not by any sense of resentment at his confinement, but by the first winning hand he'd had in the last hour or so.

"Sit and down and play the game, will you?" he barked at his friend. Chipper laid his cards down for Maps to inspect, and Maps beamed as he placed his hand on top of Chipper's.

"Deal again. That's one in a row for me!" Maps quipped. Chipper failed to see the funny side; his mind sidelined by the commotion going on outside the tent.

"It looks like someone has been hurt," Chipper explained.

"Another one?" Maps replied.

Chipper explained that this looked like a nasty one, but Maps was too engrossed in the card game to be particularly bothered. People getting hurt was, to be fair, an almost everyday occurrence at the school.

"Damned fine-looking aeroplane," Chipper noted.

Maps got up to look and agreed that it was indeed a damned fine-looking aeroplane. Such was Maps's interest in aeroplanes that normally he would've been out there examining it, but he was in the moment brooding over his confinement and plotting his friend's downfall at cards.

Chipper slowly lowered the flap of the tent and returned to the card table.

"Damned bad show for the commander," Chipper offered his opinion.

"Bad show?" answered Maps. "It serves him right for keeping us on the ground!"

Chipper agreed with his confined colleague, "It won't be long, they'll need us for something soon enough." Maps hoped so as well.

Appointments

The doctor, Victoria, the commander, and Sir Winston's secretary had a meeting to discuss Sir Winston's injury. The doctor was genuinely concerned that his patient was likely to try and get up before it was healthy to do so. He asked Victoria to keep a close eye on the patient and to be as attentive as she possibly could be. Victoria nodded her approval; she was sure that the nursing staff would be able to manage.

The commander agreed with the doctor adding that the sooner Sir Winston was back in London the happier both he and the school would be. He also said that the nursing staff must remain very discreet about the goings on at the school. Victoria noted the comment for later use.

The secretary, however, disagreed. Sir Winston needed to be active, the secretary argued. He was that kind of man. After much discussion, the four parties agreed that Sir Winston should be assigned a single nurse for the duration of his stay; primarily to keep him someone familiar with whom he could chat, but also, the commander believed, to keep the information flow about the school controlled.

Sir Winston liked the familiar and any disturbance to his routine, over and above the government's work, would put him on edge. The secretary suggested that Victoria should be his personal nurse since they appeared to get on so well. Victoria rolled her eyes and was about to complain, when the commander suggested that Victoria could be just the fillip Sir Winston needed.

The commander ordered that a room be made ready should Sir Winston wish to carry out his official duties. The secretary concluded the meeting by thanking all present and all hoped that Sir Winston would make a speedy recovery.

The commander stopped Victoria once the others left the room and proceeded to explain his thinking. He was confident that Victoria would do a splendid job and assigning a single nurse to Sir Winston would be for the best. He didn't want any nasty rumours entering the ears of Sir Winston.

Victoria reluctantly agreed to the conditions, although she would once more have to spend time alone with someone she had little interest in spending time with. She reflected that this was, in all probability, the life of a nurse.

The meeting over, Victoria set about her task. She found Sir Winston propped up in his bed reading a newspaper, his leg elevated slightly and his ankle sporting a bright white bandage.

"Please come in, young lady," he said as Victoria approached.

"How is the pain?" she asked.

Sir Winston complained of a little discomfort but said that he was otherwise fine. A little small talk followed. Sir Winston then cut to the chase.

"Have you ever thought of working at the heart of government?" he asked betraying an admiration for the young nurse he found most unexpected. Victoria found the question surprising but, on reflection, not entirely out of character.

Sir Winston explained that the government needed hard working young people to help it move along. Victoria always assumed that the government was run by public school boys, the type that always wore the right necktie. She had to admit, however, to being fascinated by the offer. Under any other circumstance, she thought that she would have jumped at the opportunity. Right now, however, she sadly concluded was a time to be right where she was, helping the people of the school, helping the very people she had grown to like, by and large. People she loved to work with and was proud to call colleagues.

"Gosh, Sir Winston," she exclaimed. "All I know of politics is what I have picked up from my father, and he is no politician."

"A bright young girl like you, will pick it up easily, trust me," Sir Winston argued.

"But I don't have a vote!" Victoria thrust. Victoria's father had often spoken of universal suffrage over dinner and tried to install in his children that the idea wasn't sound. Victoria often noticed her mother's eyes rolling whenever the subject came up. She was convinced that men shouldn't be the sole conveyors of power in the land, but her views on the subject had rarely been heard. Yet, now in this moment, the time seemed correct and the person she was with could actually do something about the situation.

"Well, not yet, but it won't be long," Sir Winston parried.

"I will work for you when I'm able to vote, is that clear?" Victoria commented once more, striking Sir Winston in the ego. "Do you think we would be in this mess if the moderating voice of an intelligent women had been listened to? It's all fun and games to you men, not to mention a very profitable venture for the ruling classes. Meanwhile, it's the people that pay the price for your decisions."

"That is quite enough of that, young lady," Sir Winston retorted trying to reestablish himself on the high ground. "You will be on my staff and that is final. It's not your position to question the authority of a knight, is it?" When questioned, Sir Winston had found it very convenient to pull rank on the lesser mortals that hadn't been honoured by the head of state.

"But I'm a nurse. How do you expect that I could so easily change direction?" a deflated Victoria replied. She was determined not to be at the beck and call of a privileged and rather opinionated simple man, regardless of his stature in society and his endorsement by a monarch she hadn't met and never seen.

"Not quite a head nurse or a leader of a large team of medical experts yet, are you?" Sir Winston replied.

Victoria was aware of what he was getting at. As a volunteer aid detachment nurse, her prospects weren't brilliant. She had ambition and achieved much in her short time in the medical profession, and she gratefully received the help and assistance of many, most if not all she was proud to refer to as friends. Yet, despite her obvious talents and skills, she would still require the approval of her peers in the hospital. In short, she wasn't in a position to abandon her dreams for a position as a simple ornament for the enjoyment of Sir Winston.

Sir Winston assured Victoria that he would personally see to it that she was made welcome and was used to her full potential.

"Besides, nursing could wait until the war had ended," Sir Winston assured.

Victoria considered the proposal for a few more seconds before once again politely declining the offer.

"Do you understand what I am saying?" persisted Sir Winston. Victoria thought that she knew, but Sir Winston wasn't in the habit of taking no for an answer.

"I could always employ you as my personal physician. My work is very stressful," he explained, hoping it would help.

"Do you fall over a lot?" Victoria asked, adding in an uncharacteristically sarcastic tone. "In the course of your stressful days?"

Sir Winston had to admit that falling over wasn't part of his daily routine. "But you can't be too careful!"

Victoria agreed that, in this moment, his care was important but tried to explain that her place was here with her friends and colleagues. Indeed, Victoria found the experience of being away from home and in contact daily with people she mostly admired and cared for was joyful. She had never, in her young life, been happier. She felt useful and was determined to continue to plot her own course.

"Fine, it is settled then. I will arrange your transfer as soon as I'm back on my feet," Sir Winston announced. Victoria was confident she was in command of where she wanted to be and no amount of pressure from anyone would put her off her course. She was just about to tell her patient in no uncertain terms about her plans when dinner arrived.

As Sir Winston ate, Victoria began to hatch a plan.

"Sir Winston?" she asked.

"Yes," replied the portly knight.

"If I give your offer some serious consideration, would you do something to help me out?" Victoria continued.

"Of course, I would," beamed Sir Winston.

"What do you know about the secret aeroplane?" she asked.

Sir Winston almost choked on his dinner. "My dear lady, how on earth do you know about the secret aeroplane?"

"The whole village is awash with stories of this aeroplane, and besides, it's in the national newspapers," Victoria explained. "And I have two colleagues who bravely helped save the crew of the secret aeroplane from certain death. These two colleagues are now punished for their immense bravery." She explained how Maps and Chipper guided the aeroplane to a safe if rather bumpy landing, and they are now being confined to their quarters as a result – a punishment that was quite unwarranted for their actions.

"I was aware of a recent incident involving the secret aeroplane, which two colleagues are these?" Sir Winston enquired.

"They are two trainee pilots named Medlicott and McGraw, sir. We, however, all know them as Maps and Chipper."

Sir Winston was aware that here had been an incident involving the secret aeroplane but knew nothing of the people involved. He was intrigued by the problem, and keen as he was to have Victoria on his staff, he agreed to investigate the case as soon as he was able.

"Confined to camp, you say?" Sir Winston asked.

"Yes, sir, confined to camp! Security risk, apparently," Victoria replied.

Sir Winston knew a little more than he was saying; he was aware of incident and had been somewhat instrumental in the punishment. It was he who determined that these two pilots were a security risk.

"Unfortunately, these two men are a security risk," he explained. "Despite what you read in the papers."

"Or hear in the market, the public houses, the churches and the dining halls and hospitals." Victoria replied.

Sir Winston considered this information, probably for the first time. He knew that there was an investigation ongoing within government, yet right here and right now his purpose was clear: he wanted to get himself and Victoria back to the big city and the heart of government.

Sir Winston pondered his dilemma momentarily. It was a sticky spot, yet he had dealt with much worse in his long and colourful career.

"I will do whatever I can for these young men, as long as you promise to give my offer serious consideration."

"I promise you, I will think it over very seriously," Victoria lied.

Sir Winston once more assured Victoria that she could happily leave it with him. Tea arrived, was poured and drunk.

Victoria tucked Sir Winston in and left to formulate an escape plan.

Sir Winston was somewhat perplexed by the thought of two men confined to camp for helping the crew of a much-prized aeroplane. He initially suggested that the two men should simply be sworn to secrecy.

"I will have to damn well see why the commander went against my orders!" whispered Sir Winston. A steward was called, and a message given. Sir Winston commanded the commander to his bedside. Victoria smiled; her plan was beginning to succeed.

"Please keep this entirely to yourself; we don't want any more news of this incident creeping out."

Brandy

The commander was having a very pleasant dinner with his wife when a note arrived. He tried to explain to his wife that Sir Winston needed his presence urgently, but she was having none of it.

"He simply has to whistle, and you come running!" she argued.

The commander explained for the umpteenth time that it was always his duty to be on duty; that is why he was the commander. His wife explained that she had seen so little of him recently and that it was all getting a little bit too much for her.

"And why is there always a nurse involved somewhere?" she added with venom.

The commander grabbed his coat without explaining any further and made for the door. His wife made her way upstairs to hunt for a large suitcase.

The commander was met at the hospital by Victoria, who silently escorted him to Sir Winston's bedside. Victoria then left the commander and Sir Winston to their conversation, drawing the curtains around Sir Winston's bed and pretending to leave. This was a conversation she wanted to hear and so she hid herself behind the curtains, her ears as close as possible to the conversation.

Sir Winston was sure he was alone with the commander.

"I want that nurse on my personal staff," he began.

"You would like Victoria on your personal staff! I can't possibly allow that," protested the commander.

Sir Winston explained that it wasn't a request he could refuse; Victoria was coming to London with him and that was final.

"Make the arrangements, and do it quickly," he instructed.

Behind the curtain Victoria seethed.

The commander if-ed and but-ed with Sir Winston for another twenty minutes, before he finally got the message.

"I had hoped to not be losing the sunshine of the camp quite so quickly," the commander stated.

"Don't worry," Sir Winston consoled. "She will be the sunshine of the government soon."

Sir Winston finished his piece and asked for brandy to be brought to his bed. It had been a long day and he needed a nightcap. The commander felt obliged to join him. Sir Winston rang a small bell that he had been given to summon assistance. Victoria crept to the door and pretended to open and close it.

"What can I get for you?" Victoria asked peering around the edges of the curtain.

"Brandy please," Sir Winston ordered. "You do have some in your office, don't you?" he asked the commander.

The commander explained to Victoria that there was a little brandy in the bottom drawer of his office desk. He emphasized the word little hoping that Victoria was clever enough to understand.

"Would you mind fetching it?"

Controlling her anger as best she could, Victoria agreed to the demand if the doctor would allow it.

"This is a matter of state," Sir Winston barked. "Now get the brandy before I have to."

Victoria's predicament was complete; however, she remembered that she still had a single card left to play.

"Will you discuss Maps and Chipper whilst I am gone?" she asked. For all of her frustration she was convinced that she had these two aging men exactly where she wanted them.

"Maps and Chipper?" questioned the commander.

"Oh yes." Sir Winston pretended to have forgotten. "Those two pilots, they are called Maps and Chipper, aren't they?"

The commander explained that Maps and Chipper were nicknames. Medlicott and McGraw were their given names.

Victoria felt she had directed the conversation enough and left to retrieve the brandy, stopping on the way to ask the doctor for instruction.

"The commander's brandy?" she asked the doctor.

"Of course, that will be fine," he responded. The doctor then grabbed his long white coat and made his way to Sir Winston's bedside. If there was brandy to be drunk the doctor that he had better be there … just in case, and just in case there was any going spare!

Arriving at the commander's office, Victoria was surprised to find the commander's secretary still at her desk.

"Can you help me find the commander's brandy?" she asked.

"The commander's brandy?" the secretary questioned. "Nobody touches the commander's brandy!"

"It's for Sir Winston and the commander, purely medicinal you understand." Victoria explained.

The secretary softened her approach when she heard the name of Sir Winston. "I guess it must be important," she giggled.

"It is," replied Victoria. "Can you also get me Medlicott and McGraw's files? They wish to discuss the case over their brandy."

The secretary opened the commander's bottom drawer. There lay two bottles of brandy and a bottle of whiskey. Reaching in, the secretary retrieved a half empty bottle.

"They will need the full one," explained Victoria.

"But that's the commander's best brandy," explained the secretary.

Victoria was encouraged by the information and encouraged the secretary to hand over the best brandy.

"Now, just the files and I will be gone."

The files were retrieved and with her hands full of brandy and papers she left.

Over the next few hours Sir Winston and the commander began to find some common ground. Both agreed that the commander had indeed the finest brandy to be found in the local area. Victoria noted that the conversation had turned in a more amicable direction. She chose her moment to thrust Maps and Chipper's files under their noses.

"Here are the files you asked for, sir," she said as she presented the files to Sir Winston.

"Files?" replied Sir Winston. "What do I need these for?"

The commander looked disbelievingly at Victoria.

"You were to discuss these two with the commander, as I recall," Victoria instructed.

"So, I was," Sir Winston replied flipping the cover over and inspecting the contents.

The situation regarding Maps and Chipper was, however, not so easily agreed upon. The commander, who since the incident had heard of little other news, was determined to keep the two pilots away from the public. He was particularly inclined to keep Chipper away from everyone; he had more than enough of that young man. He also had more than half a mind on keeping Victoria exactly where she was, but Sir Winston wanted Victoria to become part of his team in London, and these two seemingly unspectacular student flyers were firmly standing in his way.

"You have a week to think about replacing that young nurse, and releasing those two young men," Sir Winston slurred.

"I don't think my mind will change on either issue," the commander replied.

Sir Winston then explained that, given that he was here to inspect the camp, a poor report could have serious repercussions for the commander's further career. The commander swallowed hard, yet a plan was beginning to formulate in his mind.

"Perhaps," the commander started, "Maps and Chipper could be removed to a place where talk of the secret aeroplane would be of no consequence."

"Good idea!" replied Sir Winston. "Where would you send them?"

"Well, they are excellent pilots and it's about time they both saw a frontline airfield," the commander replied.

"Send them into battle ... are you sure they're ready?"

"I've rarely seen a better crew than Maps and Chipper, and I'm confident they would excel at the front."

"This would leave Victoria free to come to London to work on my staff," Sir Winston delightedly remarked.

"Indeed," replied the commander.

The Forward Defensive

Early the next morning Victoria was summoned to the commander's office.

"I understand that you're to be assigned to Sir Winston for personal duties," the commander began. "I trust that you have discussed this position with him and are happy to go?"

Victoria shuffled uneasily in her chair. "It hadn't been my plan to go with Sir Winston," she replied.

"Well, Sir Winston was adamant about it." The commander explained that there appeared to be little he could do to prevent the appointment.

"But I am happy here," Victoria pleaded. "Even if that means that I'll have to suffer dinner with you again."

The commander chose not to dwell on the word "suffer" in Victoria's answer, choosing instead to tell her what a mistake he had made, and to assure her that it wouldn't happen again.

"I love my work here, I get along with most people including Maps and Chipper, and I'm finding it easy to make many friends. Losing all that to go to London to be Sir Winston's trophy is not something I find entirely acceptable."

The commander explained that both Maps and Chipper were shortly to be assigned to the front.

"The front!" she bellowed. "Why?"

"It appears that they have seen too much, and the only sensible place to send them – somewhere they would not be asked about the secret aeroplane – was the front."

"But I have also seen the secret aeroplane," sobbed Victoria. "It is all over the newspapers!"

"That's different," explained the commander. "The news you read can be controlled. Actual sightings and casual talk could put the whole project in jeopardy."

Victoria appeared to understand the logic, but accepting the facts would be a harder task.

"Besides," the commander continued, "if you really are going to work with Sir Winston in London …"

"Sir Winston?" Victoria interrupted. "I'm going wherever Maps and Chipper are going, even if that's to the front."

The commander was startled by her reaction; he hadn't realised that her bond to Maps and Chipper was quite so strong. On reflection, however, he later admitted that it was probably entirely in character. All three had arrived at the school at the same time and, apart from that one nasty incident that resulted in the commander having to discipline Chipper, they appeared to be extremely happy.

"What I was going to say, before you interrupted me," the commander spoke once more. "was we must be able to find a way or come to a compromise with Sir Winston."

The commander and Victoria sat in silence for a few moments, trying to think of a way out.

"Perhaps you should all go to the front," the commander suggested. "Sir Winston cannot possibly have any objection to three patriots wanting to serve their country."

"The idea is clever but a little extreme," replied Victoria. In any case, only qualified nurses were allowed to be so close to the front.

"You won't actually be going to the front. If I know the type of man Sir Winston is, he will never sanction such a move." The commander then relaxed in his chair and a small self-satisfied smile drifted across his face.

"It's worth a shot," Victoria said, hoping that the commander was a better judge of men than he was of women.

The commander thanked Victoria for her time and ordered her back to the hospital. "I had better accompany you and tell Sir Winston the good news." A driver was summoned and the two were driven the short distance back to the hospital.

Victoria stepped down from the car and thanked the commander. Inside the hospital, she found Nellie enjoying a cup of tea on the veranda.

Nellie was a regular nurse. She had become a nurse almost three years ago, and Victoria looked up to her, because she appeared to be always in command of a situation and was never flustered. Nellie was from the south coast of England, from a place only thirty miles from Victoria's hometown. She was, however, rather plump. Her rounded face gave her a kind and approachable demeanour; her rounded and full figure gave her a sense of self-doubt that all around her found difficult to comprehend. The dichotomy between her personal and professional faces was stark. Victoria found her to be the professional, competent and thoroughly likeable person she would like to be. Nellie found Victoria to be the English rose that she always wanted to be. The two got on famously.

The commander straightened his uniform and swept past Nellie as if she wasn't there before making his way to Sir Winston's bedside.

"She's going with them!" Sir Winston was not at all pleased with the outcome. The commander had to spend several minutes listening to Sir Winston ripping his management technique to pieces. Sir Winston soon found, however, that no amount of shouting at the commander would persuade Victoria that London was the place for her.

"Bring her in here. She'll listen to me!" Sir Winston announced proudly.

The commander turned and left the bedside, where he eventually found Victoria chatting with Nellie.

"He wants to talk to you," the commander explained.

Victoria excused herself and reluctantly followed the commander back to Sir Winston's bed.

"It is death and destruction over there, peace and tranquility over here. Why won't you see reason?" Sir Winston enquired.

"Would I rather be a hard-working dedicated nurse helping the common soldier overcome his wounds, or be a trophy for your work cabinet?" Victoria decided to pull out all the stops.

Sir Winston tried to explain that trophies weren't allowed in his work; he simply wanted to accelerate her career path. He hoped that she would see the sense and maybe one day step into the political arena herself.

"Politics needs keen minds and able bodies," he told her.

"I will enter politics when I have the conviction to enter politics, and when women are allowed to vote, and not at the whim of a particularly unsightly cabinet secretary."

While Sir Winston was shocked at the bluntness of this young lady, it was a trait that he found particularly attractive in women. "Now look here, young lady," he barked. "You are coming to London and that's final."

Victoria scowled at Sir Winston. "I'm going to the front and that's final, even if I have to walk there myself." Holding her head high, Victoria turned and left the bemused Sir Winston to his thoughts.

The commander was quickly summoned to Sir Winston's side. "This camp is an undisciplined shambles," he announced. The commander found that a little difficult to take but nodded gracefully.

The commander calmed Sir Winston down and then explained that neither of them wanted to see Victoria go to the front with Maps and Chipper.

"But if they go, she goes," he explained. As a volunteer, she was not at the whim of military protocols.

"She is a strong-willed young lady," Sir Winston added.

However, the commander explained, if he didn't have to send Maps and Chipper to the front, then Victoria could stay where she was. She could even be in attendance if ever Sir Winston needed her assistance.

Sir Winston agreed that, as a compromise, it wasn't too bad an idea. "But what will we do with those two pilots?"

"We could always send them to an aerial ambulance brigade. I understand that there is to be one set up to transfer the injured from the front back home," the commander said, offering his own solution.

"What a splendid idea," Sir Winston replied. "But they will need wings won't they?"

The thorny subject of pilot's wings was looming for the commander.

"If they are ready, I will present them before I leave."

"They would like that," the commander lied.

"In the meantime, what you need around here is some team spirit. You need to foster some camaraderie," Sir Winston announced changing the subject. The commander was bound to agree.

"The accident rates amongst the students are the lowest in the country; it's the instructors who seem to be the problem."

The commander studied the figures and knew Sir Winston to be right.

"What sort of things do you do to encourage the instructors to bond with the students?" Sir Winston asked. "Students and instructors seem to be the opposite ends of the stick in this establishment."

The commander agreed; he had little option. He told Sir Winston that all ranks' parties and dances were often arranged, although sadly they were often poorly attended. Sir Winston was shocked.

"Parties and dances!" he screamed. "This is a military unit, not a dance hall." Sir Winston then suggested, rather forcibly, that a military unit should be focusing on team games and strategic quests, not dances and parties. "You won't see too many men at the front sipping sherry and dancing a polka!"

Once more the commander dutifully nodded.

"What this place needs is a game of cricket!" Sir Winston announced.

"Cricket? That's a bat and ball game, isn't it?"

"Damned right it is!" Sir Winston was obviously quite a fan of the game.

"Get a game organized," he instructed. "The students will play the instructors, and you and I will attend as honoured guests."

All was settled. If it's cricket he wants, then cricket he will get.

A thoroughly disheartened commander turned and left Sir Winston's presence, where Victoria met him at the doorway.

"Why don't you just go to London with him?" the commander asked. "It would make life so much easier for all of us."

"Would you?" replied Victoria.

The commander could see her point and decided to leave it at that.

"The maniac wants us all to play cricket," the commander added. "That is the price of getting you out of going with him."

"You did it!" shrieked Victoria.

The commander explained that Maps and Chipper were to be awarded wings and transferred to an aerial ambulance unit. Victoria leapt with joy and hugged the commander for a short time, before sense returned and both looked embarrassed at one another.

"However, if ever Sir Winston needs you, he will be able to arrange a visit and you will be his personal nurse."

"Did you promise that?" Victoria asked.

The commander nodded. "It was the only way," he added.

For the rest of the day the commander had to try and learn a little about cricket, he also had unsettling task of telling Maps and Chipper about their prospects on an ambulance unit.

Maps and Chipper received the commander's latest summons as they awoke from an afternoon snooze.

"Good grief, what does he want this time?" Chipper asked.

"He wants to us both together, so I guess it will be about the secret aeroplane."

Both agreed that it would be a simple meeting, and both hoped that common sense prevailed and they would be free to leave the camp at any time. They both got dressed and walked over to the commander's office. Stepping inside the office, Maps and Chipper both observed the sullen face of their commander.

"There is no easy way to say this," he started, "but you were both to be sent to the front as soon as possible. However," he continued, "in order to prevent Victoria from becoming an unwilling part of Sir Winston Winston-Frobisher's team in Whitehall, he has assigned both of you to an ambulance squadron."

"What about our flying?" Chipper enquired naively.

"They are flying ambulances," the commander informed the two pilots. "You will be ferrying injured troops back from the front to the hospital here."

"But Victoria will be in London," Maps sobbed.

"Have you been listening at all?" the commander asked. "Victoria will be staying right where she is." Maps's face immediately lightened; Chipper almost giggled with joy.

"This ambulance thing will be no picnic, however," the commander commented. "You will be flying daily into the hottest areas on the frontline. It will take bravery, skill and dedication."

"Do either of you know how to play cricket?" the commander continued.

Maps and Chipper, puzzled, looked at one another. Maps said he had played a little for his local village team.

"Good," exclaimed the commander. "Get a student team together. You will be playing the instructors next week." He then dismissed the pair.

The meeting was simple. That was it: an announcement, an invitation, and they were gone. Outside, the consequence of what they had been told began to sink in.

"Cricket?" questioned Chipper.

"Cricket," replied Maps. "We had better go and see what equipment there is."

Talk of flights to the frontlines would come later; right now, there was a game to organise. In the dark recesses of a small shed, hidden behind a large lawn mower, a bag lurked. It was a big bag held closed by a large brass clasp. The bag had obviously been there for some time as it took the full might of both Maps and Chipper to pry open. Fortunately, they found what they were looking for inside. Chipper pulled out and then held up three straight pieces of wood that puzzled him somewhat.

"Those are stumps," announced Maps.

A further delve into the bag revealed two bats, one still smelling of linseed oil, and a collection of half a dozen cricket balls, all neatly stitched together and looking very nearly new.

Propped against the wall behind the bag were a set of large polls and nets that would serve very nicely as practice nets.

Suitably satisfied with the find, Maps picked up one of the bats and proceeded to waft it around as if playing authentic cricket shots. "This is excellent equipment," he proclaimed. "We better get the lads together and see who can play and who can sit it out."

"I would prefer it if I could sit it out," Chipper proclaimed.

"Sit it out? You are my right-hand man in this adventure. I want you on that pitch fighting it out with me!" Maps explained.

"Like a couple of blokes in an aeroplane high above the front." Chipper's mind was suddenly refocused on the realities of this morning's news. "Don't we all have to dress in white?"

That evening all of the students gathered in the newly erected nets for practice. Maps organised the small group into players and non-players. The non-players were to be used as a last resort. Maps hoped that there would be more than enough players to make a team.

Maps asked Chipper if he would mind volunteering to be the first to enter the nets to practice his batting. Chipper nervously agreed. Maps showed him how to strap the large pads to his legs, and how to correctly hold a cricket bat. Chipper waddled away with the large pads catching each other as he walked. He still had a curious object in his hand, a sort of elongated object that he had no idea what to do with. Maps wandered over to his friend and whispered to him that the object was a box.

"What do I do with that?" he asked. Maps casually told him to use his imagination before he walked away.

Instruction given, and the box firmly in place, a very nervous Chipper walked awkwardly to the far end of the nets, whilst Maps looked for an experienced bowler to bowl a few balls at him.

Towards the back of the bunch of students stood "Fast" Freddie. No one really knew what the nickname was all about, but they all called him Fast anyway. Maps instructed him to bowl a medium speed ball down to Chipper, and Chipper would undoubtedly smack the ball many a mile into the distance. Maps had been to many a net session and knew what to expect.

Fast Freddie cleared the area, and after a fashion began his run, getting faster and faster until with a great leap and a single motion he bowled a medium paced ball to Chipper. Chipper had raised his bat a little as Fast Freddie approached. He watched the great leap and thought to take a step forward, as he had been instructed. Sadly, by the time he had lifted his front foot, the ball had crashed into the stumps behind him, the ball coming to rest in the bottom of the net.

Fast Freddie, happy with his work, paced towards a now shaking Chipper to offer the young batsman a piece of advice.

"You may want to move a little faster next time," Freddie explained in a polite yet somehow menacing tone.

"Be a little more gentle with him, will you please?" Maps asked Fast Freddie.

"That's why they call me Fast," Freddie replied. "I used to play for my county before this lark came along." Indeed, Freddie had played at a very high standard. His six-foot-four-inch frame with huge shoulders and muscular thighs were the features of a very fine fast bowler. Freddie was both an exceptionally fine bowler and a very competent aeroplane fitter.

At the end of his run once more, Freddie steamed into the wicket and let another fast ball go. This one Chipper saw. As it whistled between his arms and stomach, Chipper suddenly felt rather scared.

"Are you alright there?" shouted Maps.

"Fine," Chipper lied in reply.

Maps decided that Fast Freddie was a player and would definitely be on the team. Looking around Maps spotted another big lad, Sparky Timkins. He was one of those new electrical technicians, but he also possessed the all the features of a fast bowler. Maps threw him the ball. Sparky examined the ball expertly before giving it a vigourous rub on his trousers. Suitably polished, he transferred the ball from one hand to the other and with a skip and a jump he began his run. Chipper watched intently as the bowler approached the stumps and watched with nervous, jittery eyes, as for the first time Sparky delivered the ball with a great leap. On leaving his hand, the gathered players gasped as they heard the whistle of the wind as the ball passed through the air. Once the ball had pitched, it reared up and before Chipper could move out of the way it impacted with crunch on his nose. Chipper threw his bat to one side and sank to his knees. Sparky smiled the cruel smile of an executioner.

Freddie and Maps came running to Chipper's assistance. Maps looked at Sparky, and before he could ask, Fast Freddie informed him that not only had Sparky also played county cricket, but that there were few better fast bowlers in England than him. Maps gulped and shouted for someone to call a medic. Chipper was instantly thrown into shock; his skin became pale and he began to feel very, very cold. Maps found a blanket and placed it around him. Freddie strode purposefully back up the wicket toward Sparky; he patted his fellow fast bowler on the back before telling him that the spectators at Gloucester would have enjoyed that.

The news quickly arrived at the hospital, where Victoria and Nellie were resting a little between pointless bouts of activity with Sir Winston. As quickly as she could, Victoria ran to collect her first aid bag, whilst Nellie made sure that there was a bed for the poor unfortunate new patient. A car was found and soon Victoria and Nellie were being raced over to the cricket pitch.

Maps greeted the two nurses and, without his normal calming demeanour, he rushed them over to see to Chipper.

"Chipper!" shrieked Victoria. "What have they done to you?"

Maps explained what happened whilst several of the now shaking cricketers carefully lifted Chipper to his feet. Victoria absorbed all the facts before she looked Sparky directly in the eyes and screamed.

"You are a perfectly beastly brute!"

Sparky smiled once more. Never one for flattery, Sparky later concluded that Victoria was indeed correct, and he liked that. Fast bowlers for time in memorial had been a heartless bunch of men.

Soon Maps, Chipper, and the two nurses were in the car and being hurried to the hospital. The shock of the accident was passing over Chipper, allowing the pain to creep through. Every stone or rut in the road made him grimace in pain, the larger stones made him cry out in pain. Each cry was a dagger through Victoria's heart. At each grimace Nellie repeated the same old mantra.

"You men play such silly games." Deep inside Nellie, however, was the quiet satisfaction that for the next few days she would have some sensible male company in the hospital. She was becoming tired of the constant chatter of young women and the moans of the older male patients.

The doctor was soon in attendance and didn't like the look of the injury. "Broken noses," he explained, "are tough injuries to fix." The doctor did the best he could before he ordered Chipper to bed rest.

The bruising was spreading rapidly across Chipper's face. Soon his eyes and his ears would be blackened and his face distorted to the point where even close acquaintances would find it hard to recognise him. Maps and Victoria left Nellie at Chipper's bedside to complete the paperwork. Both recognised that this accident would be the talk of the school by the morning.

Nellie comforted Chipper as best she could. The two nurses carefully removed the cricketing equipment from around his person before completing a bed chart. They tried to keep Chipper as quiet and relaxed as could be expected. She took his blood pressure and, with a reassuringly steady hand, took some blood.

Sir Winston snored intermittently that night as he slept restlessly in the bed next to Chipper, who moaned and groaned with every turn of his head. Sleep didn't come easily for either of them. Nellie kept an all-night vigil at the two men's beds.

The sister in charge of the ward was a formidable woman, large in frame, wise and commanding in stature. She was used to a crisis and often thought that she would like one or two more crises around the hospital. This situation was right up her street looking after a sick Knight of the Realm and a young pilot.

"Victoria!" the sister screamed. "Take charge of Sir Winston. Nellie, you look after young McGraw."

Victoria was saddened that Nellie was made Chipper's nurse. She really wanted to look after him, and as they were in adjacent beds it would have been easy enough to look after both of them. However, the sister had spoken and it was beyond her to complain.

Cricket practice resumed the next evening, Maps was busily trying to find a volunteer to bat in Chipper's place. To his surprise none were forthcoming, so he took the bat himself and prepared to face the combined terror of Fast Freddie and Sparky Timkins. Soon, however, normality returned. Sparky and Freddie met their match. Maps proved very skilled with the bat, driving and cutting the two bowlers with an aplomb that both bowlers grudgingly admired. The more Maps swung the bat, the faster the two bowlers bowled. All three were soon enjoying themselves so much that they failed to notice their colleagues melting away into the evening. It wasn't long before the light became too dim to see the ball and the cricket for that night was packed up and stored. Tomorrow evening it would be the turn of the instructors.

In the early hours of the morning, Chipper was still moaning and groaning. His pain was too much for Nellie to bear and she went over to his bed to comfort him. The bleeding had fortunately stopped, but the bruising around his nose, eyes and mouth was heavy. Nellie looked at his face and tried to imagine what he used to look like. She noticed his hands clenching and unclenching as the spasms of pain took hold and then subsided. Taking his hand in hers, she could feel the tension in him. Nellie remained with Chipper until the spasms stopped, when she could finally unclench his hand from hers. Standing up she looked down on her patient and smiled a very loving smile.

Maps arrived at the hospital before breakfast the next morning.

"May I see him?" he asked Nellie.

"For a short time, but he needs to rest," Nellie explained.

Nellie escorted Maps through the corridors of the hospital. Past each ward he could hear the groans of patients in pain. Soon enough, Nellie and Maps were at Chipper's bedside. Maps looked at him and cringed.

"I'm so sorry, old friend," he tried to explain.

Chipper opened his bruised eyes as best he could and before speaking he winced with pain. Nellie reached out and again grasped his hand. Chipper's eyes opened once more and he tried to speak, but the words failed to come out.

Nellie replaced Chipper's hand on his chest and she and Maps retired to the staff room, where Victoria was making them both a nice cup of tea.

"It's only a cricket game," said Maps.

"It may be only a game, but we already have one in hospital. How many more will there be by next week?" Then Nellie offered her opinion. "Damned silly game, if you ask me," she grumbled once more. "There is a perfectly good bowls green nearby. Why can't you play a sensible game like bowls?"

"Bowls is for old men," Maps explained.

Victoria could see how right Maps was. Her father was quite the bowls player back home.

Maps then told Victoria all about the impending move to the ambulance unit. Victoria announced that she had volunteered for the front, but for the foreseeable future she had been asked to remain at the school. Nellie could find no sense in the appointments of either friend, but wished them both luck anyway, adding that the cricket game would be a nice way to send Maps and Chipper off to their new unit.

"If they were both in a fit state," Victoria added with a grin.

Nellie then suggested that the nurses should all pitch in to help making teas for the cricketers. Maps thought this a wonderful idea. Victoria wasn't so keen but eventually agreed to the plan.

Over the next few days, Nellie and Victoria attended as best they could to Chipper and made plans for a tea fit for their departing heroes.

The Mission

Baron Barduffloss wasn't happy. His pilots were volunteering for all manner of other duties. The desertion started when he explained the nature of the task they were training for. He was down to his last three pilots and two of them were not terribly keen.

Barduffloss and his immediate superior needed a meeting, and urgently.

On the train to the meeting Barduffloss reviewed the plans and had to admit to himself that it was unlikely that so many aeroplanes could make it, but if he could maintain a small force of about four aeroplanes, he could maybe just carry it off.

Barduffloss and Hans sat at the dinner table and began to discuss the plan. Hans was considered something of a whizz at this flying game. Having learnt to fly early on, he had risen to great heights in the flying establishment. Sadly, he lost a leg in flying accident the previous year. This impediment didn't, however, diminish his passion for flight.

The plan seemed simple enough: fly over to England and disrupt the building of a secret aeroplane. The devil was, however, in the detail. Secret Wood was 120 miles from the coast, the Castle was 300 miles from the opposite coast and there was about forty miles of water between the two coasts. At a rough estimation, that made 460 miles of flying. The aircraft flown by Barduffloss and his men was good for about 300 miles, with one person on board and no extra weight.

Hans and Bardufloss discussed the lack of range and the lack of manpower, and both agreed that both were a problem. Bardufloss, however, wanted to agree on solutions not problems. Bardufloss and Hans thrashed out the problems over an exceptionally fine dinner washed down with an equally fine wine. After such a fine meal, the solution became more and more obvious.

The solution agreed on was, in fact, the only viable solution. Bardufloss and his team would have to fly to the coast, refuel, then fly the remaining distance at the most economic speed. The disruption would have to be carried out with the minimum of equipment, unless he could persuade his pilots to lose an amount of weight that they could ill afford to lose.

It was decided, as the report suggested, that the secret aeroplane appeared to be made of wood and fabric, so a combination of fireworks and matches would do the job. To set off the fireworks, the aeroplanes would have to land on the airfield. Hans and Bardufloss then had to consider a time for the flight. A nighttime adventure would be out of the question, as the navigation and fuel would both be questionable in daylight, let alone at night. Therefore, the best time for a landing on a British airfield would be at about three o'clock ... time for English tea! If they glided in, no one would ever hear them. *Brilliant!* thought Bardufloss.

Bardufloss was eager to return to the castle and make the final arrangements. A pat on the back and parting good luck, sent a cheerful Bardufloss speedily on his way.

***

Chipper was all bandaged up and in a chair on the veranda when Maps next came to see him. Chipper decided not to get up for his friend, as that would be decidedly against Nellie's strict instructions. He was after all only on the veranda because Nellie had caved into his constant demands.

The veranda overlooked the expanse of the cricket field. From the woods beyond, the birds sang out their impeccable chorus of song and screech. Occasionally, a cat could be seen creeping through the undergrowth until it spied its prey, when it would stand motionless until the prey fell into the exact position to be devoured. The veranda was a lovely place and would be even more so had it not been for the pain of a broken nose and the accompanying bruising.

"How are you?" Maps asked.

"Fine," Chipper fibbed. "The swelling is subsiding, the bruising is reducing and, if all goes well, I shall be as right as rain in a week or so."

Maps looked down at his seated friend and judged that with all that swelling and bruising, a week was at the cutting edge of optimism. "Bloody bad luck that cricket ball smashing you in the nose," Maps announced wistfully.

Chipper wasn't all together in agreement with Maps's appraisal of his situation. "Bad luck?" he replied. "That bloke tried to kill me."

"Still, it got you out of spending an indeterminate amount of time in the tent. I have been bored to the point of tedium," Maps confided. His words may have been directed at his friend, but his mind was in another place altogether.

Victoria was making tea for her patients when she heard Maps chatting with Chipper. She quickly smartened herself up, finished the tea and placed it neatly on a tray. She then, trying to look as professional as possible, strode purposefully through the ward towards the veranda. Placing the tea tray on the table beside the injured Chipper, she pretended to attend to Chipper's nose.

Her mind was, however, far from the most focused. Suddenly being with Maps made her somewhat nervous. A single word from Maps and Victoria flinched, catching Chipper's nose with her finger. Chipper let out a yell at the sudden pain but had the presence of mind not to offend Victoria with the expletive or two that he would probably have normally uttered at such pain. Victoria apologised and sensing Chipper's discomfort she retired to a safer distance.

Maps could sense Victoria's uncomfortable feeling; he prided himself on being able to sense when a lady needed a way out. Maps decided to engage her in more conversation. "Cricket match, heh," he announced.

Chipper groaned again at the thought of that damned sport.

"I have the cricket teas already organized," replied Victoria. "There are cucumbers, and salads and chopped pork, and my special dish for you all. Oh, you'll help me, won't you Maps?" Victoria's excitement appeared genuine, but she had other motives for her excellent tea.

Victoria had heard of affection and love from various friends and relations, but she didn't exactly understand precisely what it was. But, if love existed, she was somewhat expecting she would feel it for Maps. *But what of Chipper*, she wondered. Chipper was also in her thoughts as often as Maps was. Oh, the confusion, a confusion that she was certain only a professional approach would resolve.

"Teas," she announced. "You will help out, won't you?"

"I would be honoured," Maps said kindly accepting the generous invitation. "What is the special dish?"

"I thought rabbit stew," replied Victoria enthusiastically.

"That will have the chaps in raptures," Maps said offering an opinion he had no right to offer on the behalf of his dearest friends and colleagues. Rabbit appeared with monotonous regularity in the dining hall, and Maps considered that the men would be heartily sick of the sight of rabbit stew.

"Oh fantastic," Victoria enthused. "I can hardly wait."

Her enthusiasm was infectious, and in their excitement, both went for the tea tray that remained on the table beside Chipper. They clashed heavily and the tea tray slipped from the table spilling its hot contents over Chipper's lap. Chipper once more resorted to yelping wildly; he could sense that expletive on the tip of his tongue, but he swallowed it. Victoria was horrified that she had inflicted yet more pain on Chipper and rushed to wipe the hot tea from his lap. In her haste, she misjudged the distance and the crown of her head impacted Chipper's nose and finally that expletive found its way out.

"Gosh!" screamed Chipper.

Underpreparation

The boffins in the secret shed in the Secret Wood were having a crisis meeting.

"I tell you it's overweight, overstressed and just can't take the weight!" bellowed boffin number one with a frustration borne of constantly not being listened to.

Boffin number two concurred. "It's a great idea, but we just don't have the technology to make it work!"

The ministry official was, however, having none of it. It was the aeroplane that would bring the troops home by Christmas, although once again he failed to tell them which Christmas. The idea that a big aeroplane could take troops to wherever they were needed and quickly, appeared to be a great idea. The ministry knew that the aeroplane would be excessively big, and they knew that it would require a special type of pilot to fly such a big and fast machine. In preparation they had built an enormous factory in which the machine would be built and commissioned the best pilots in the land to train other pilots. Vast sums of money were spent on the buildings and training the people to build such a cutting-edge machine. All problems had been explored and overcome. All they needed now was an aeroplane to put into production.

The boffins weren't too impressed with the pleadings of the ministry. They could see the plan, the idea and had done everything they knew, but it was just not on. The aeroplane wasn't ready and, short of a miracle or two, it was never going to be ready.

Inside, the secret sheds was the third prototype version ready to fly. With bigger engines and a more streamlined shape, next to it were the remains of the second prototype. Boffins poured over the remains, attempting to find out what went wrong. Every now and then they would summon the pilots who would for the umpteenth time explain what happened. Investigators continued to claw through the wreckage looking for the single fault that would prove or disprove the pilots' recollections. The ministry would, by and by, call the boffins for a progress report. The higher echelons of the cabinet were eager to get to the bottom of this accident. The prime minister demanded answers from tired and weary cabinet secretaries.

Through the night the boffins and the ministry team discussed and finalised a report. They – to be fair, mostly the ministry – concluded that given a few more test flights it could work. The new prototype looked promising; all the new technology available to the boffins had been included. It was equipped for both the rocket assisted takeoff and the bungee take-off options. The cockpit was updated with all the available instrumentation necessary to give the pilots all of the information they needed to fly it. It was even finished with a very thin metal covering that assisted both in cutting drag to a minimum and crucially offering protection from fire.

The aeroplane was painted in the most elegant colour scheme. All the boffins were sure that given a modicum of concord between them and the ministry, the new aircraft would be the fastest machine in the skies, if only it would fly.

The boffins did still worry about things the ministry weren't interested in: things like weight, lift, drag and stress. It was all simple mathematics to the ministry team, an unnecessary tedium that they endured whilst trying to get the boffins to roll it outside and fly it!

Breakfast next morning was a tired affair. The boffins still had a long day ahead, and the ministry team had a train ride back to London. Before they left for London, the ministry team asked to see the test pilot. Chilly Chilton was duly awoken and over a nice cup of tea the smiling, happy and content ministry team put their findings to him.

"If you think I am getting back inside that death trap again, you have another thing coming!"

A shocked ministry team looked at the pilot.

"Not for all the tea in China," Chilly added.

The pilot became more and more animated as the conversation carried on.

Finally, the opinion of the test pilot was noted by the ministry; it would be point forty-nine at their next meeting. The test pilot went back to bed and tried once more to ignore the pain from the burns on his feet and hands.

The ministry had spoken, however, and a new pilot had to be found and quickly. Whilst the search was on, the boffins and their helpers pushed the new prototype from it hangarage into the bright morning air. Its coat gleamed in the early morning sun, and all stood back from the machine to marvel at their creation. The aeroplane reflected the sunshine into the boffins' faces before a wheel under the weight of the engines was seen to sink into the ground. Then the wheel on the other side also sank, and finally, the tail of the mighty machine struck the grass and broke. Chilly Chilton then arrived at the scene and breathed a huge sigh of relief. Today was to be a day without flying.

Victoria was having an equally bad morning. She was trying to get Chipper to eat some food, but he seemed determined to keep his distance. Victoria found this most disheartening and a little unusual. Perhaps Nellie would have more luck. Nellie was summoned and her bright cheerful face settled Chipper a little.

Soon Chipper was eating porridge and feeling much the better for something in his belly.

"Perhaps you had better see to everything he needs from now on," Victoria conceded with a heavy heart.

Nellie agreed that it was a good idea and a pleasure for her as well. Chipper smiled.

Engagement

The best part of a week passed by and Chipper's moaning became less as the bruising and the pain subsided. He began to enjoy the company of Nellie and the taste of the porridge she brought him every morning.

The morning soon arrived when Chipper felt well enough to slide from his bed and walk around a little. Nellie observed from a distance, smiling to herself at the progress. Porridge was served, and Nellie encouraged the young pilot to walk some more.

"It's not like you have a broken leg or anything like that," she chirped as Chipper found a pair of slippers and strode around the room, becoming more confident with each step. Nellie smiled at him with each step, and occasionally Chipper would smile back in her direction. After half an hour or so, Nellie offered the opinion that Chipper was in a condition where he could walk around the grounds of the hospital. Chipper beamed at the thought and Nellie beamed back at him.

By mid-morning, Maps had collected Chipper and was walking him through the woods on the opposite side of the cricket ground. The team had been announced the previous evening. Maps was to open the batting for the students, an honour he bestowed upon himself as he was the only player to have survived uninjured after facing an over from Fearsome 'Fast' Freddie. He claimed it was down to luck that all of Freddie's deliveries had missed him, but Chipper rather suspected that Maps was quite handy with the willow bat in his hands.

They carried on chatting as they passed through the trees. Maps commented on the wonderful smell of the woods, before remembering that Chipper was perhaps not in a fit state to be appreciating smells. On the other side of the woods, they turned left and sat by a fence watching a training aircraft taking off and landing. The sounds of the reciprocating engine, blipping and going silent on approach, was pleasant enough to hear, but they both longed for a chance to fly again.

"What do you know about these ambulance aeroplanes?" Chipper asked.

"Not much I am afraid," Maps explained. "They are a new thing in the flying corps."

Maps surmised that they would be large aeroplanes, and consequently rather slow. Both men hoped that they would be two-seaters, for safety and companionship. Chipper believed the job would be very tough; after all, hospitals rarely have landing strips attached to them. Maps agreed but was sure that they would be flying into and out of prepared frontline stations.

The delights and dangers of a new challenge were looming for them both, and both felt they were neither ready for the challenges ahead, nor prepared.

"What do you think it will be like?" Maps asked Chipper.

"I really have no idea, but if I were to hazard a guess, the word terrifying would come leaping to my mind," Chipper replied.

"Oh, don't talk like that, old boy. I know that we will still fly together, and we will be fine as long as we are together." Maps strangely felt, as so many did, that he was a survivor and he really thought he could protect his friend.

"I wish I was so certain," Chipper replied. "However, with you in the back to protect me, I'm sure we will have a damned good fighting chance."

"That's the spirit!" Maps replied enthusiastically. "And when I am flying, I can rely on you to keep me safe."

Maps began to walk a little, and Chipper followed as best he could.

"Have you been to a flying station over there?" Chipper enquired.

"Yes," Maps told him. "Once or twice when time allowed, I would visit a local flying station and chat to the people there."

"Did you like them?" Chipper added. "I hear that the flyers aren't looked upon kindly by the troops."

Maps agreed. "Yes, that's often case. The flyers, however, have their own kinds of dangers to endure." He went on to explain, "The life of an infantryman in the trenches is simply to stay alive long enough to go home on leave. The flyers have remarkably similar ambitions. The only difference between the two are the living conditions."

"Are they really that bad?" Chipper asked.

"Life in the trenches is just about as awful as anyone could imagine," Maps told him. "Lice and rats, poor food, mud and dead colleagues – it's intolerable. Friends are a burden to the trench soldier, as you never know who will get up in the morning, and who will die on a pointless hour of sentry duty. A man can die in a myriad of ways in the trenches; the flyers are restricted to dying in only one or two ways and they largely rely on their own skill to determine which way they are going to die."

"Well, I'm very glad that I'm going to an air station and not the trenches," Chipper said, giving his opinion.

Maps agreed wholeheartedly with him. "Besides," he explained. "The airmen do have a much more comfortable existence."

Maps explained that the airmen on the continent could get out of the station and explore the local area, which was often, or though not always, relatively untouched by the war. The airmen were free to meet the local women and eat and drink in the town and villages around their stations. Most evenings the officers would have a party in the mess, and these parties often included an awful lot of drinking and playing the fool.

"That sounds like a much more convivial existence. Do you think we will get much time to enjoy the life over there?" Chipper asked.

Maps pondered for a moment. "I don't suppose we will." Maps thought that the job would be a simple case of flying into a station, picking up who ever needed treatment and rushing them back to the hospital as quickly as possible.

"It sounds really interesting and challenging work!" Chipper said.

Maps agreed with his injured friend, and he then proceeded to explain the down sides of being a flyer on the continent.

"Airmen often suffered from a fear and nervousness not present in the trenches. They were driven by commanders who were overconfident in their own mortality. There were like a good horseman who were never thrown, those that knew they would stay on their mounts no matter what. Once the initial fear of their opponents evaporated, and the more they survived encounters with those opponents, the more confident they got. These leaders were so confident of their own abilities, they found it difficult to relate to simple novices and led them into dangers that, to the leader, appeared routine. Newcomers in the outfit often didn't survive the first few encounters."

"Gosh that is terrible," Chipper replied, astonished that this could happen in a modern conflict.

"Maybe that's part of the problem. The conflict is so modern that we don't know how to deal with the strains and pressures put upon the combatants."

"This mechanised warfare has our leaders befuddled and confused," concluded Maps.

Maps ended the conversation there. He wasn't so sure he was going into areas of the war that even he knew much about. He felt a duty to Chipper not to darken his mood or to undermine his natural confidence. Besides, neither of them were going to a frontline post; they were simply going to be ambulance drivers. It was time to change the subject. Finding a fallen tree close by, Maps led Chipper to it and they both sat down on its mossy top.

"That Nurse Nellie is rather sweet on you, don't you think?" Maps said, starting a new phase of the conversation he longed to have with his friend.

"She is a nurse. It's her job to be sweet on her patients," replied a flustered Chipper.

"It looks like more than a professional interest," Maps remarked. He hoped Chipper noticed the "more than a professional interest," as it may leave Victoria free to see him more often.

"She is a bit plump," Chipper replied.

"She is a fine woman," Maps announced. He continued that a healthy figure was a sign of a good cook and housewife, and she would look after Chipper in a grand style.

"Does that mean that you are dissatisfied with Victoria's slim figure?" replied Chipper hopefully.

"No, not at all," Maps replied. "Victoria is a women who looks after herself." Her figure was one that Maps admired often and dreamt about almost nightly. "Besides," he added, "she like dogs!"

"What on earth have dogs to do with anything?" enquired an irate Chipper.

"It means Victoria wouldn't be averse to a little mud or chaos around the house," Maps explained. Chipper heard what Maps was saying but really didn't understand.

"But you are the cleanest and most organised man I have ever met!" he stated.

Maps was indeed a very organised man. He had been brought up to believe that there was a place for everything, and everything should be in its place.

"Precisely," Maps replied. "Opposites do very often attract."

Chipper immediately recognised a thin excuse and began to realise the real meaning behind this conversation.

"Maps," Chipper began. "Victoria has no interest in me. She only has eyes for you, so there's no need to be jealous of me."

"I'm not jealous of anyone," Maps replied. "I would just like a little time to get to know her better, and with you and Nellie as a couple we could all enjoy evenings together and we'll never have to worry about seating arrangements."

"I see," said a sheepish Chipper. "It's all about you and Victoria. You have no need to worry about me. It's the higher command that you need to worry about. Almost everyone that visits the station has half an eye on Victoria. Generals and politicians were quite literally tripping over themselves to get into our hospital."

Maps had to agree with his friend. He noticed a marked rise in the injury rate in the last few weeks. Maps got up from the fallen tree and began to walk again, and Chipper followed closely behind.

"When we go to dinner with Victoria, shall we invite Nellie along as well?" Maps shouted.

Chipper heard Maps's comment and hurried to catch him up.

"Why not!" Chipper replied. "She has been awfully kind to me."

The two friends headed back in the direction of the airfield.

More aircraft flew the circuit, gently but noisily approaching the field before racing off for another trip around. The box-shaped wings of the aircraft could be seen flexing slightly as the controls were moved. The scarves of the instructors could be seen waving in the slipstream, and deep down the two flyers were sure that inside those cockpits there were two extremely nervous people.

Victoria had tea for her favourite two pilots ready for them when they returned. She handed a cup to Maps, placed a cup on a table, retired to a safe distance and offered it to Chipper. Chipper edged closer to the table and reached out for the cup. To his surprise, it didn't scold him, hit his nose or break. He sat himself down in a large chair and drank.

It was only two days until the cricket match; the team was in fine fettle. Freddie was exercising his arms, taking on the tug-of-war team single-handedly. The boffins in the wood gathered around yet another set of calculations. The engineers had almost affected the repairs to the burned areas of the airfield. In the woods, the birds sang, and the cats stalked, the rabbits burrowed and the foxes slept. All was well in this little part of England.

In a castle far away, the fireworks were loaded, and Baron Bardufloss gathered his men around him for the flight to the coast.

The Day Arrives

Wednesday morning on the continental coast broke bright and sunny. Having arrived the previous evening, a long sleep and a gentle awakening was the order of the day. Today was the big day. Getting dressed Bardufloss pondered the day ahead – was today to be his day? Of course it was, he mused. Bardufloss pulled back the flap of his tent and smiled at the weather.

"Perfect!" he announced to the birds, the few clouds and a rather startled sentry guard. Confident and happy he looked forward to a strong coffee and a tasty breakfast.

Bardufloss, once satisfied that he was ready for the day, went to wake his fellow pilots from their beds. The two remaining volunteers were soon up and about, stretching and doing the deep breathing exercises Bardufloss had prescribed to them.

Suddenly, an almighty commotion broke out on the airfield. Bardufloss and the pilots ran to the scene as fast as they could, and there at the edge of the field in a small revetment that housed Bardufloss's machine stood a burning aircraft. The ground staff were running around the aircraft trying to get as much water on to the fire as they could. However, the water supply was a long way from the revetment and despite their best efforts the aeroplane continued to burn fiercely.

Soon the fire reached the compartment that housed the fireworks that Bardufloss was to use for the mission. The flames licked at the fireworks and inevitably the gunpowder within them began to explode, sending all present scurrying for cover.

"That's my aeroplane!" screamed Bardufloss with anguish before he dived into a hedgerow for cover.

The other two pilots quickly retreated to the safety of a small hut and drew straws.

The loser would still be going; the winner would have to "sacrifice" his place on the raid and give his aeroplane to Bardufloss. Moments later the two pilots appeared, one happy the other not so happy. Bardufloss, true to his character, demanded the aeroplane of one of the other pilots, so the winner duly offered his.

With his mission crew now down to two, Bardufloss demanded a meeting with the personnel involved. With the fire still burning brightly in the distance, Bardufloss addressed the meeting.

"This mission is far too important to be cancelled," he began. "We now have but two aircraft and one box of fireworks."

He continued to explain to the gathered pilots that in order to meet the mission requirements the base would have to supply him with a replacement aircraft, one drawn from the inventory of the airbase. The base commander demanded to know why he should give up an aeroplane to a visiting officer.

"We are Special Forces on a special mission. The demand for an aeroplane is not a request it's an order!" Bardufloss barked with an unnatural anger.

The commander could see the logic in the request but knew that his aeroplanes were lacking in range and speed and would only hinder any operation. "But your machines are much faster and can fly much farther than our outdated machines," he explained.

Bardufloss could also see the logic in the commander's protestations but demanded to see the available aircraft anyway.

The commander escorted Bardufloss and his pilots to a hangar close by. Inside, a couple of mechanics were engaged in a game of cards when the commander approached. The commander unseen by the mechanics approached their card table and slammed his walking stick aggressively onto the table, startling the two mechanics, who immediately jumped to attention.

Around the hangar were at least five aeroplanes. All were rather ancient biplanes that, in a flyable condition, would have undoubtedly been powered by antiquated rotary engines. The closest machine, however, had no engine attached to it, the engine having been removed to form the basis for a card table. The commander questioned the mechanics about the engine's whereabouts, but both realised instantly that revealing its location would not be a good idea and so they remained quiet.

Behind this machine, another lay on its side, its wings removed and stashed against the side of the hangar. Two more lacked propellers and tail pieces, however, the final example was complete and was soon drawing the eye of Bardufloss.

"What about that one?" he asked.

Bardufloss and the commander walked purposefully in its direction, followed closely behind by the mechanics.

"What is wrong with this machine?" the commander asked.

It transpired that the machine was by any definition in perfect working order; however, the last pilot that had flown it claimed that it didn't fly in straight line.

"Not in a straight line?" mocked the commander.

The mechanics agreed that the fault report was a little odd, and they'd checked it over and found nothing wrong. The commander smiled and turning to Bardufloss suggested that his pilot should take it aloft to see if it were suitable.

Bardufloss agreed that that would be a good idea and volunteered the pilot who sacrificed his aeroplane to try this one.

The smile disappeared suddenly from the face of the unfortunate flyer, as did most of the colour from his cheeks.

The mechanics manhandled the aircraft from the hangar whilst the commander instructed the unfortunate pilot. He instructed the pilot on how to handle the torque of the aeroplane's radial engine and the flying characteristics of the aeroplane. The pilot appeared to comprehend all that had been told him.

Walking cautiously to the aeroplane, he was helped to strap in by one of the mechanics, who then, with a grin, swung the propeller. Soon the engine burst into life and the pilot took off.

Bardufloss and the commander watched anxiously as the aeroplane bounced across the grass before becoming briefly airborne. Suddenly, the wing dropped and before the commander could say "torque effects" the wing dug into the ground and the aeroplane disintegrated about its pilot.

Bardufloss and the commander were quickly on the scene. The commander was mortified that yet another aeroplane had crashed on his airfield.

"That's the fourth aeroplane this week!" he screamed.

Bardufloss was more concerned with his pilot, who was sitting upright, still strapped to his seat forty metres ahead of the aeroplane.

Bardufloss rushed to his pilot and found him gibbering in his seat. He appeared to be asking for his mother to take him to school. Soon the medics arrived and whisked the pilot off to receive medical treatment.

The commander approached Bardufloss looking a little glum at his loss.

"Thank you anyway," Bardufloss said. "I don't think we will be needing this aeroplane after all."

The commander seethed and thought to bawl this Bardufloss man out, but etiquette got the better of him. He did, however, manage to tell Bardufloss that he and his men should leave the airfield at the earliest possible opportunity, without shouting. Bardufloss thanked the commander for his hospitality and ensured him that the mission would be flown at the earliest opportunity.

After breakfast Bardufloss and his last remaining pilot went through the mission once more, checking and double-checking everything in the most methodical way. The aeroplane had barely enough fuel to complete the mission and barely enough fireworks to do any damage, but if he was successful, this was the mission that Bardufloss knew would accelerate his career. The remaining pilot didn't share his leader's enthusiasm and spent the rest of the morning hoping and praying that something would go wrong with his aeroplane.

The Umpire

Victoria was busy in the kitchen preparing the tea for the cricketers. The rabbit was prepared, and the cucumbers sliced so thinly you could see through them. Nellie had engaged herself slicing the crusts from the edges of the bread. She thought it was the done thing and was rather enjoying herself.

Fast Freddie and Sparky Timkins were jogging around the camp taking the best wishes of their colleagues and fellow players. Their large frames were an imposing sight, even if their military issue short trousers left much for the athlete to desire.

Over breakfast on the veranda, Maps and Chipper were looking forward to the game. Chipper was feeling much better and had been elected the umpire for the home team. It was a role he was more than happy to fill, because that meant he wasn't in the line of fire. Chipper had taken a little time, whilst he endured his convalescence, to gen up on the laws of the game.

"Now you do know the laws of the game, don't you?" enquired Maps.

"Oh yes, my knowledge on leg before wicket is second to none!" replied a proud Chipper.

"Well actually, I meant the real rules of the game." Maps was suddenly convinced that his umpire hadn't learnt the rules he wanted to play by.

"Real rules?" Chipper was intrigued.

Maps then took a good half an hour explaining that each team had nominated an umpire to even up the cheating that goes on. He began to instruct Chipper on the etiquette of cricket umpiring.

"Your team always gets the benefit of the doubt, as any close calls go with your team," Maps explained.

"But that's not cricket," protested Chipper.

"It may well not be cricket, but just remember which team is more likely to buy your beer after the game!" explained Maps.

Chipper got the point and sank into deep thought about how he could bend the rules a little to help his colleagues out.

Deep in Secret Wood, the boffins sat around aimlessly. They had been constantly arguing since the visit by the ministry. In the secret shed, Chilly Chilton and Bill Masters paced about as the fate of the project swung from being feasible to being madness. Chilly, as he was prone to, had his own thoughts on the matter, but his opinion would form such a small part of the discussion that it seemed silly to offer an opinion at all. He could of course jump from the aeroplane if he felt things were getting out of hand.

That Wednesday morning seemed as normal as any Wednesday morning would. The sun was shining, the woods and fields were alive with the normal Wednesday morning things, even the boys delivering papers and goods were blissfully unaware of the danger at hand, just a few miles away in a field on the English Channel coast.

In his little house in the nearby village, Arnold was busying himself preparing a light breakfast. Before him on the table was a map and the letter he retrieved from the waves. The letter detailed the Bardufloss mission with instructions on how he could help in the unlikely event that something would go wrong. The instructions seemed simple enough. Arnold was to position himself near the flying school and where necessary, and by any means possible, he was to disrupt any attempt by the school to intercept the mission.

Since his meeting with Victoria on the coast, Arnold had taken great care to investigate the area around the school. Just beyond the woods that bordered the cricket ground was a large river with a bowls green built on a small island mid-channel. Arnold had infiltrated the bowls club and was now a regular bowler. He also invested in a small boat that he used as his personal transport to and from the island bowls club.

Anticipating any hiccoughs, Arnold, on joining the club, carefully inserted into the conversation that he had a several gentleman friends who would also like to play bowls, and that they would soon be available to join the club.

Arnold found the bowls club to be an excellent place to exchange small talk with the locals. He discovered much from the chit chat he overheard during bowling games. It was in this company that he had learnt that the press reports of the crash of the secret aeroplane were correct. It was also here that he had learnt of the building of a new secret aeroplane. The conversations he listened so intently to held all sorts of details that could be pieced together to form a bigger picture.

Chief amongst his friends was a man who worked as the local milkman. Always ready with a joke or two, the milkman was keen to talk about his daily routine and chat about the places and people he had seen and talked to. Most of the information Arnold required was inadvertently given by this jovial ex-milkman.

A large, rather portly gentleman also provided good information. Nobody knew exactly what he did to make a living. His bowling could best be described as wayward. He was often the butt of groups' jokes as he bowled wildly and inaccurately. His fault lay in his loose tongue, and when it came to the running of the club, this trait often found him in hot water as far as the club were concerned.

The retired mathematics teacher was good for information about the number of boffins at the Secret Wood. He taught most of their children and was constantly bemused by either their brilliance or their indifference to calculus. The maths teacher was excellent at integrating new members of the club.

The rest of the bowlers were apparently rather mundane. A couple were ex-Army members and often dictated the discipline of the group.

One rather remarkable fellow was an ex-diplomat … perhaps. He purported to have travelled the world from Haiti, through Siam to Hong Kong. His stories of exotic travel and the people he encountered were often met with an enthusiastic response but were more than often a repetition of a story regaled time and time again.

The group all got on well together particularly when the bowls were packed away and the beer began to flow. Arnold would spend many hours with this group and he mostly enjoyed the experience.

But for all of the enjoyment, the bowls club was work for Arnold. He mentally noted everything he heard and would often spend many hours until late into the night copying conversations into his notebooks.

Arnold believed that the island was an ideal place to observe the upcoming mission. From the island he could view most of the sky above the school, and on a cloudless day he could see as far as the Secret Wood on the other side of town. His boat offered a means of transport that was flexible, silent and capable of carrying several other people.

Flight

Bardufloss called "CONTACT."

The propeller of his borrowed aeroplane was swung. The engine coughed and spluttered and finally with a jolt that shook the whole aeroplane, it burst into life. Bardufloss looked up at the fuel indicator on the top wing and smiled with satisfaction that it had indeed been filled to almost overflowing with precious fuel. He glanced to his left to see the same process being carried out on his colleague's aeroplane. That aeroplane also coughed and spluttered, but the jolt didn't happen. A second time the coughs were heard and the splutters seen, but still no jolt. An engineer was called, and the engine began to be dismantled. Bardufloss watching this and seeing his fuel disappearing pointlessly, drove his aeroplane into wind and advanced the throttle. The aeroplane gathered speed, and Bardufloss looked across at his disabled colleague and saw the crowd that had gathered around the aeroplane all smiling and waving. Bardufloss grunted joylessly to himself and allowed his machine to carry him onward to the clouds.

Soon over the English Channel, Bardufloss prepared himself for the long flight over southern England. He checked and double-checked almost everything he could check and double-check. He monitored speeds, heights and fuel consumptions. He listened intently to the aeroplane about him and felt satisfied that even in this intensely stressful moment his aeroplane seemed fine and was flying beautifully.

"Play!" called Chipper, and the sport began.

The captain of the instructor team was a tall and athletic sport instructor. He tossed the ball from one hand to the other whilst contemplating his first move, eventually throwing the ball to the instructor team's best bowler, Dan "Chucker" Cowans. Maps tapped the toe end of his bat nervously on the crease, while Victoria arranged things on the table nervously. The student team sat nervously in their seats fidgeting and chattering. The game was about to burst into life.

Chucker Cowans walked purposefully to his carefully measured bowling mark before turning and running towards the pitch. With a great leap, he delivered a thunderbolt of a delivery that Maps didn't even see, let alone hit. Maps did, however, smell the leather as it passed perilously close to his nose. Victoria gasped at the sight, alarmed at the first delivery. Maps took a split second to reclaim his poise before pretending to play a classical shot, after which he leaned on his bat and stared in the direction of the bowler. Looking cool and calm, Maps then wandered down the wicket, prodding and poking at the grass, looking to flatten the lumps and bumps that he knew would assist the bowler every time he delivered the ball.

The next two deliveries were also thunderbolts. One passed so close to Maps's ear that he could hear the whistle of the air passing around the seamed ball. Maps resolved to be calmer; he knew he had been lucky so far. The next delivery was a toe-crunching yorker that Maps tried desperately to avoid. The ball crashed into Maps's leg pads, directly in front of the wickets.

"HOW IS THAT!!!" screamed the bowler, looking directly at Chipper whilst throwing his arms in the air with excitement.

Chipper paused for a moment and looked at Maps. Both he and Maps knew that the ball was out, and it looked out, and it was by any stretch of the imagination the most out a batsman could be without him looking around at the shattered stumps of a bowled batsman. Maps moved his hands to his lips imitating the motion he would make when drinking a beer. Chipper watched the action, took a deep breath and looking intently at his dearest friend he announced to the field NOT OUT!

Bardufloss, meanwhile, passed the Cliffs of Dover without pausing to admire them. Skirting around London he set a northerly course. All was well in the aeroplane: the engine hummed rhythmically, the fuel was being guzzled at a slower rate than expected, and Bardufloss beamed behind his cotton scarf. All was well with the mission and mentally Bardufloss could already hear the applause he would receive upon his return.

The Secret of a Good Rabbit Stew

Victoria sat back in her chair by the makeshift pavilion, jealously guarding the cooking pot that contained her rabbit stew. The smell of the stew made her very happy and very hungry. She was absolutely sure that this would be the best stew anyone ever tasted. Nellie attended to the tables that were set out in front of the pavilion, making sure that each had sufficient paper napkins and jugs of water. In an effort to both support and show solidarity with her nursing colleague, she made herself as busy as she could make herself. Finding all that could be done was done, she went to see what help Victoria could use.

"You could sort out the scones."

This request pleased Nellie to no end as she was from the west country and thought she knew a thing or two about scones. Reaching for the jam, she was about to start when Victoria interrupted her.

"Cream first!" she advised.

"Not where I come from," Nellie explained.

The two ladies then spent a few moments, moments they really didn't have to debate the order of cream and tea. Finding no satisfactory agreement was ever going to be had, Victoria relented and let Nellie get on with what Nellie knew to be correct. With all the scones spread with jam, Nellie found the clotted cream and started to add a dollop or two onto each scone while Victoria looked on and rolled her eyes!

Sir Winston Winston-Frobisher was determined that he should see his ideas in action and summoned the commander. The commander was a little disturbed to soon find himself pushing the knight's wheelchair, advancing the knight across the uneven terrain that lay between the hospital and the pavilion. The commander wasn't pleased at finding himself in the role of a porter, a job he felt he shouldn't be seen performing. The knight's needs must be met, however, so he put his back into the task as best he could.

Sir Winston chattered constantly on the journey, telling the commander what a great idea he himself had and if the commander put his mind to it, he would also one day achieve high office. The commander nodded in agreement and thanked Sir Winston for his kind words. The two stopped at the edge of the cricket pitch to observe Sir Winston's cricket match. The picture was exactly the way Sir Winston imagined it, and with a pleased, rather self-satisfied grin he ordered the commander push him around the boundary to the pavilion.

"What a glorious day for a game of cricket," Sir Winston said beaming.

Out in the middle, Maps had overcome his nerves and was now clattering the opposition bowlers to all parts of the field. Down at long leg, Chucker Cowans was still brooding about Chipper's decision to give Maps a "not out," and his anger increased with every swipe of Maps's bat.

Victoria felt a sense of pride in her friend's heroic innings. She applauded as the sound of the ball on the bat rung around the field, but occasionally she dashed back into the pavilion to stir the stew. Nellie remained behind the table, gazing at Chipper. She thought he looked marvelous in his long white coat and black trousers, even if the large plaster that covered his nose made him look a little comical.

Maps sent another ball crashing to the boundary before the captain of the instructors signalled to his star bowler. Throwing off his jumper, Chucker Cowans came running to the middle to collect the ball, which he proceeded to rub vigourously on his trousers. Like an angry bull, he stood at the far end of his run and glared intently at Maps. Suddenly, and with an exaggerated skip, he was into his running. His arms were pumping at his side and the sweat from his brow flowed like rain behind his head. He leapt hugely into a delivery stride and with a great swing of his arm the ball was on its way down the wicket. Maps, now brimming with confidence, took a stride towards the ball and, with a flick of his wrists, he sent the ball crashing into the square leg boundary. Victoria jumped from her seat and applauded the magnificent stroke. Chucker Cowans stood in the middle of wicket, hands on hips and glaring even more intently. Maps smiled politely back at the bowler, which only served to enrage Chucker even more.

The captain of the instructors approached Chucker Cowans and offered him a few words, designed to defuse the situation. His attempts, however, fell on deaf ears. Chucker grunted a little, turned and walked back to his mark.

Chucker's next delivery was a brute that pitched short and bounced before travelling in high and fast towards Maps's head. Skillfully, Maps swayed out of its way before he strode down the wicket to tap his bat on another imaginary lump in the pitch. The last ball of Maps's innings was equally evil – it reared up into his chest. Maps got the edge of the bat on the ball, the edge diverting the ball away from his body, but straight into the hands of a fielder. Maps looked up at Chipper, and Chipper looked back at Maps, but it wasn't his call to make. Maps tucked his bat under his arm, saluted the star bowler with a doff of his cap and trudged slowly back to the pavilion. Chucker and the captain danced a little jig in the middle of the pitch.

Maps removed his protective equipment and went to consult the scorer. The scorer was an elderly and slightly shortsighted man who was a barber by profession, but due to his shortsightedness had seen his business decline in recent years.

"How many did I score?" Maps asked him.

"Well, it could be either 98 or 102," admitted the scorer. "I didn't quite get the signal in the previous over."

"Let's call it 102," Maps pleaded.

The scorer amended the score accordingly and Maps became the first batsmen to score 100 runs in an inning for the flying school. Sir Winston applauded Maps enthusiastically, demanding the commander to bring the young man over to him.

Sir Winston commended Maps on his fine innings before asking maps if he would like to play for the team that represented his government department.

"It would be an honour," answered Maps.

After a few minutes washing the sweat from his face and hands, Maps's next port of call was the pavilion to help Victoria with the rabbit stew, where she suddenly become deeply engrossed in conversation with Sir Winston. Maps's happy face dropped at the sight of his beloved Victoria and the amorous Sir Winston deep in conversation. Maps made a beeline for the two determined to put a stop to Sir Winston's shenanigans.

"Excuse me, Sir Winston," interrupted Maps. "I trust you will not be requiring Victoria for dinner this evening, as she is already engaged."

Sir Winston took a pace back. He had never been spoken to so bluntly and by such a lowly man before. But it was summer, the sun was shining and he really wasn't in the mood for an argument.

"Why, certainly not young man!" Sir Winston apologised. "After the ear-bending she gave me last time I asked her to join me, I would welcome a peaceful and restful evening!"

Victoria, Maps and Sir Winston regarded each other before breaking into a polite giggle.

The inning was quickly ended, and the hungry players were soon all sitting at tables awaiting the main course. Maps and Victoria walked amongst the tables and served the most splendid rabbit stew ever served at a cricket match, whilst Nellie offered her delicious cucumber sandwiches. Having finished their duties, Victoria and Maps sat on opposite sides of the table next to Chipper and Sir Winston. Nellie joined them sitting opposite Chipper. All enjoyed a fine lunch in very agreeable company.

Small talk was still being exchanged when the sound of an approaching aeroplane was heard.

"Gosh, that one is low!" exclaimed a startled Chipper.

"And fast by the sounds of it," Maps added.

Suddenly, the noise became intense and a strange looking aeroplane flew low overhead. Maps and Sir Winston watched the aeroplane go over before continuing dinner. After a short pause, the general caught Maps's thoughtful gaze.

"Did you see what I just saw?" Sir Winston asked.

"I think so," Maps replied.

"Bloody strange markings on that aeroplane, weren't they? I wonder who on earth painted an aeroplane like that. We could use a painter with an eye like that to paint the aircraft around here," Sir Winston announced.

"Are you sure it is one of ours?" Nellie asked.

"Of course it is," Sir Winston announced. "The war is too far away to interfere with us here."

Bardufloss was close to the point where he calculated he should be climbing to begin his glide into the Secret Wood. He checked and then double-checked his instruments, his engine readings and his fireworks. With everything in good order, he cut the engine.

A Firework Display

The boffins were just finishing their meeting. The kettle was on and about to boil. Only one subject remained: Future Development.

"I have a strange suggestion that might help our lift problems," announced boffin number seven.

The room turned to look at the slightly embarrassed looking boffin. He knew he would be out on a limb with this, but with the kettle whistling merrily away in the corridor, he carried on regardless.

"If we put another engine on the roof, pointing upwards with a huge propeller ... we would get the benefit of the downdraft from that propeller as well as the wings and engines!" he excitedly explained. "Maybe we could reduce the take-off distance substantially."

There was a slight silence as the idea sank into the boffins' heads. Followed by a further, slightly longer pause, as the idea mixed around with all the other brilliant ideas that revolved around in the heads of boffins. The silence seemed interminable to boffin number seven; he held his breath and awaited the inevitable ridicule.

The words from boss shattered the silence. "Young boffin! That is the most ridiculous idea I have ever heard! The propeller, I estimate, would have to be so big that it would cut down any trees that stood nearby!"

Boffin number seven's head bowed and he dropped into the depths of despair. How would he ever be able to contribute an idea again?

"That's right," ridiculed another boffin. "People would start calling it a chopper!"

The room erupted into fits of laughter. Boffin number seven got up and left the room with his tail firmly between his legs.

"Chopper!" laughed his colleagues. "It'll never catch on!"

Boffin number seven just made the door when something caught his slightly tearful eye.

Bardufloss had his eyes firmly on Secret Wood and the landing strip. He could finally see the secret aeroplane. He noted that it was huge, however, it also looked extremely fast.

My, that looks fast! boffin number seven muttered to himself as the something that caught his eye materialised into an aeroplane.

Bardufloss checked and double-checked the compass, the airspeed and the altitude and carefully monitored his gliding descent into the field. He smiled to himself when he saw that he had, as expected, achieved total surprise.

The instructors had a delightful lunch, and it was with a happy heart that they occupied their seats to enjoy the afternoon's sport. Maps followed big Freddie onto the field. Freddie was raring to go, and he was baying for the instructor's blood. Sparky Timkins stood close by with an evil look in his eye. Fast Freddie was soon at the end of his run, putting the instructors' opening batsmen firmly into his sights.

Maps gesticulated wildly with his arms, moving fielders from one position to another, pushing them backwards and forwards as if they were chess pieces. Finally, when Maps was happy, he pointed to Fast Freddie and retired to a safe distance. Freddie acknowledged his captain's signal and began his run up.

As Freddie leapt high into his delivery stride an almighty bang was heard. Startled Freddie spun in midair in the direction of the noise, his outstretched arm catching Chipper squarely on the nose. Chipper squealed, Nellie shouted, Victoria gasped, and Maps ran to his friend's assistance.

Bardufloss leant into his bag of fireworks once more, and lighting a match on the sides of his trousers, he fired off a rocket bounced off the sides of the secret aeroplane. Bemused by this unexpected turn of events, another rocket was lit and fired, and again it bounced off the aeroplane.

Boffin number seven ran toward the intruder and tried to get as close as he could before he would attempt to rugby-tackle the man. Bardufloss saw him coming and swerved to one side, leaving the boffin lying nose down on the grass.

The path between the aeroplane and himself cleared of obstacles, Bardufloss ran quickly towards the gleaming aircraft. The flyer was in need of a new plan and quick. Running aimlessly toward the huge aeroplane Bardufloss scrambled about in his bag, hoping to find another firework. Grasping the last one in the bag, he transferred it between his teeth and then set about looking for a match.

Noticing that the large cargo door on the side of the aeroplane was open, an opportunity finally presented itself. Bardufloss leapt into the aeroplane and was initially staggered by the sheer size of the it. This caused him to hesitate for a moment before noticing the boffin approaching once more. He had no more time to waste. Bardufloss lit and placed the firework, pointing it towards a large tank that filled the rear of the aeroplane's interior. Then he leapt from the aeroplane through the open door, straight into the arms of the oncoming boffin.

The boffin was knocked to the ground as Bardufloss raced across the airfield towards his own aeroplane. This was when the commotion was finally noticed by the guards in their little hut. Running into the open, they were confronted by the sight of a prostrate boffin, and a man running towards a very strange but fast-looking aeroplane.

Sadly, in their hurry, the guards neglected to pick up any weapons with which to apprehend the criminal, and then there was an almighty explosion that broke the back of the secret aeroplane and was so loud that everyone was knocked off their feet. Barduffloss was only meters from his aeroplane when he was sent flying to the ground. He quickly, however, regained his senses and made his getaway as fast as his aeroplane would take him.

The explosions could be clearly heard from the cricket field, and as the noise increased, the tension amongst the players and spectators increased. The game came to a sudden halt as the sound of the huge explosion reached the players. The instructors, sensing imminent danger, ran as they could to the woods to hide. Sir Winston dived into the nearest tented accommodation and slid deftly underneath a bed. Victoria remained firmly rooted to her spot, determined to protect what was left of her stew. Nellie gasped and, dropping everything, sprinted onto the field to help Chipper.

Whilst Victoria stood motionless, apparently deep in thought, she remembered the strangely painted aeroplane that flew low overhead, not twenty minutes before. The school team, seeing the panic of the more seasoned professional soldiers about them, also ran, but to a more substantial-looking concrete hut.

Victoria, suddenly gripped with a medical calling, started running towards the still screaming Chipper, catching Nellie on the way. She grabbed Maps by the collar and the two of them, one running and the other desperately trying to find some legs, ran to assist their fallen colleague.

As they reached Chipper, the sound of a fast-approaching aeroplane was heard.

Maps thought quickly; the commotion all around him suddenly disappeared and he stood to see the strange aeroplane nearing the cricket field. Maps ran to pick up a bat and then ran to pick up a ball. Holding the bat in his sweaty hand, he threw the ball to Victoria.

"Quickly Victoria, take aim and gently throw the ball at my bat!" he ordered.

The gentle nurse tripped clumsily over the prostate body of Chipper who once more yelped with the pain. Regaining her balance, she managed to catch the ball Maps had thrown.

Victoria carefully took aim and gently tossed the ball at the bat in Maps's hands. Maps watched the ball arc from her soft and caring hands through the air. He could see the seam turning as it arced its way towards him. With a great heave of the bat, he struck the ball. The ball left his bat with a crack that reverberated around the entire county. The instructors appeared at the edge of the wood to see the flight of the ball. The school team craned their heads around the side of the hut. Sir Winston eased himself from under the bed only to find that he had caught his braces in the frame of the bed and was stuck.

The ball made a gentle whistling sound as it made its way skywards, its trajectory seemingly on course for the strange, but brightly coloured aeroplane. The ball carried on and on but appeared to be losing momentum. At the final moment when it looked for all the world as if it would fell the lone aeroplane, the ball reached its apogee and began to fall earthward. Maps looked horrified to see that his best efforts were in vain. The instructors all retreated into the woods with a groan. Maps's felt that this was no time to sulk over his missed shot and ran to catch the descending ball. In a vain attempt to make the catch, Maps dived headlong towards the ball but missed it. He ended up lying on the ground with a mouth full of grass.

Victoria had, however, seen another bat lying on the crisp green grass. She picked it up and shouted instructions to the prostate Chipper. Chipper had another ball in his white jacket. He fumbled slightly but eventually found the ball, grasping it firmly and holding it aloft. Victoria signalled Chipper, and he tossed the ball in Victoria's direction. With a mighty swing of the bat, Victoria connected firmly with the ball.

The ball left her bat at speed and whistled skyward. The instructors again appeared at the edge of the woods and watched as one at the trajectory of this second missile. Maps spat the grass from his mouth and turned to follow the flight of the ball. It appeared to be right on course, but did it have the legs.

Bardufloss was busy in his cockpit, checking and double-checking the direction home. He looked up to see that his glide allowed him just enough fuel to get home. He began to relax and enjoy a job well done, when suddenly Bardufloss's world was turned upside down. He heard a thud, then a crack, then an overrevving engine. Instinctively, he checked the instruments and dials in the cockpit. Finding nothing immediately amiss, he looked up and checked the aeroplane. The wings and tail seemed fine, but the propeller had begun to come apart. Bardufloss concluded that one of the blades had been reduced to a length that was somewhat less than optimal.

Victoria jumped up throwing the bat high into the air as she saw her shot had hit the propeller of the strange aeroplane. Maps saw it too, and he ran to embrace her. Then the strange aeroplane went suddenly silent and began to head earthward. Chipper raised his bruised head to view the action and was cracked squarely on the nose by a carelessly discarded cricket bat. He screamed the scream of the century as the bat bounced off his nose and landed with a thud at his feet.

The school team ran from the hut, the instructors ran from the woods and Sir Winston appeared from under the bed, looking slightly dazed.

Chipper lay almost motionless groaning.

A Bad Job

The events of the day affected many people in many different ways.

Arnold spent most the early afternoon playing bowls at the island club. A pleasant game was proceeding normally when the first explosion was heard.

"Another one gone down," said one of the bowlers, referring to the large amount of, and his familiarity with, aeroplane crashes.

Arnold, on the other hand was well aware of the significance of this particular noise. Excusing himself, he made his way quickly to the exit and boarded his little boat. Setting sail towards the noise, Arnold rowed with a passion he rarely had. He was aware that the bowls club was in all likelihood very close to the scene of any potential crash.

Standing dockside, his friends moaned and complained that he hadn't completed his game. It was considered very bad sport to not finish a game. They consoled themselves by ending the game and retiring to the bar for refreshments.

The boss raised his head on hearing all the commotion that had broken out around him. The aeroplane had long gone off into the distance. All that remained of its visit was the burning wreck of the government's finest aeroplane.

At the school, instructors and pupils wandered around aimlessly looking for someone to lead them. Sir Winston immediately took charge of the situation, ordering a team of students to apprehend the occupant of the downed aeroplane. Sir Winston had always been of the opinion that orders should be short, simple and easily understood. He was convinced that this situation demanded all the qualities of his orders. The guards would thank him later.

Shortly afterward, the instructors began to emerge from their hiding places in the woods. Cautious of another aeroplane in the vicinity, they looked around and tried to spot one. Then satisfied that the coast was clear, they made their way to the middle of the field to congratulate Victoria.

The instructors tried to hoist Victoria onto their shoulders but were rebuffed by her.

"Will you all please stop this nonsense!" she pleaded with them.

Chipper still lay groaning in the grass, Maps was slowly picking himself up and Nellie was standing mid-pitch gesticulating at the aeroplane. Chipper groaned once more, a groan that snapped Nellie out of her anger.

"Victoria," she screamed. "Chipper is down!"

Victoria and Nellie were both soon by Chipper's side. The nice white plaster that they had so lovingly applied to Chipper's nose had turned red. Nellie cradled Chipper in her arms and told him that everything would be alright.

Having reassured him, Nellie turned to the instructors who gathered around the scene. "Stop that gawking," she hollered. "Go and get a cart and a doctor."

Soon enough Chipper was lifted onto a cart and was on the way back to the hospital. Sir Winston stopped the procession as it neared the pavilion. "A damned fine show you put on there, young man," he congratulated. "All of you young people should be proud of yourselves." It was only then that he noted that the wheelchair wasn't with him. "I appear to be cured!"

The assembled crowd beamed at him, and then returned Chipper to the hospital, where the doctor was waiting.

With the wounded and self-important all safely dealt with, the guards led as many as would follow towards the field where smoke from a large fire was rising.

Arnold arrived at the scene of the crash before anyone else. Burning in the field were the remains of a very fine aeroplane, and staggering around the field was the aviator. Arnold cautiously approached the pilot and shouted the secret word. Bardufloss stopped in his tracks on hearing the word. He knew that it meant something but was unable at that moment to grasp quite what it was.

With no time to lose, Arnold grabbed the pilot and hurried him off to the nearest cover, where the pilot discarded his flying overalls. The two men hid in the cover of the trees for several minutes whilst Arnold calmed the pilot down and explained the plan. Bardufloss may have been a master of all things aviation, but his proficiency in other languages was far from perfect, so Arnold told him to keep his mouth shut and allow him to do any talking.

The plan was simple and soon it was put into effect. Walking a short distance up the road, the two men leaned on the top rung of a farm gate that was a short distance from the scene of the crash. It wasn't long before the two observed the advance of a party of obviously military men and hangers on.

The guard party marched smartly past the two men without thought to question their presence. Following closely behind the guard was Sir Winston, who had taken the opportunity to accompany Victoria.

Victoria spotted the two men and, finding the face of one slightly familiar, she greeted them kindly. Arnold returned the greeting whilst Bardufloss's gaze remained fixed on the scene in the distance. Two or three paces further, Victoria stopped then turned towards the two men.

"Don't I know you?" she asked.

Arnold mumbled a reply hoping that no more would be said.

"Didn't I see you at the seaside a few days ago?" she persisted. Sir Winston urged her forward, but Victoria was having none of it.

"We shared a crab sandwich as I remember," she carried on.

"Crab sandwich!" screamed Sir Winston. "We have work to do. You can discuss lunch with your friends afterwards. Now move along."

Victoria thought to obey Sir Winston, but there was something about this familiar face that troubled her.

Arnold's heart rate began to climb. For the first time since arriving in the country, he felt a genuine sense of anxiety. That anxiety was heightened when Victoria asked him about his friend.

"He is hard of hearing and since he suffered wounds at the front. He's never spoken to anyone." Arnold hoped his feeble explanation would keep Victoria from enquiring further.

Victoria accepted the explanation and, after offering her sympathies to the young man, she returned to Sir Winston's side and walked off into the distance.

The guard party soon arrived at the scene of the crash. Parts of the aeroplane were still smoldering on the ground, while small fires burned the vegetation in the general area. Surrounding the aeroplane, the guard party awaited a higher authority. Sir Winston soon arrived at the scene, having asked Victoria to remain at what he considered a safe distance.

Sir Winston and the leader of the guard party entered the cordon and proceeded to examine the wreckage. The remains of the wreckage yielded very few clues. The fabric so admired by Sir Winston had burned through. A seat was still somewhat recognisable but there was no pilot in it.

Sir Winston ordered the guard to assemble a party to look for the pilot.

"What should they be looking for?" the guard asked.

Sir Winston suggested they look for tracks or items of burned clothing. The guard did as he was ordered and so it was, and with little enthusiasm, a small party began to scour the grass field.

Sir Winston found the remains of the engine; embedded in the ground, it offered few clues.

"It looks very odd," the Guard commented, adding that it wasn't like any engine he'd ever seen. "Are you sure it's one of ours?" he asked.

Sir Winston began a long lecture about how it couldn't possibly be anything other than one of theirs, this far inside the country. He continued to explain his reasoning when a motor car arrived on the scene.

From the car alighted several men in white coats carrying clipboards. The leader of these men strode forward menacingly. "What do you think you are doing?" he screamed at those already there. "Stand back from that aircraft. It may not be one of ours."

The guards, who long since concluded that it wasn't one of theirs, smirked to themselves as Sir Winston berated the boffins in their white coats. He reasserted his position that the aeroplane couldn't possibly be one of theirs, considering it was this far inside the country.

"And just who on earth might you be?" inquired the leader of the boffins.

Sir Winston was rather taken aback by the lack of recognition and proceeded at length to inform the boffin of his exalted rank. Once the introduction concluded, Sir Winston again asserted the aeroplane couldn't possibly be an enemy aeroplane.

"But it just destroyed our secret aeroplane!" the boffin announced.

Another motor car arrived bringing Stevens, the man from the ministry, to the scene.

Walking smartly to the group of men who appeared to be in command, Stevens announced his presence with some choice words, words that a man from the ministry should never be heard speaking. Given the rather impolite opening lines from Stevens, Sir Winston felt it necessary to calm the situation. His calming words appeared to only inflame the situation.

"Who the hell are you!" screamed Stevens.

Sir Winston immediately informed this young man from the ministry exactly who he was. Stevens immediately recognised the name and his demeanour changed almost instantly. Despite the fact that Stevens felt that the secret aeroplane was his aeroplane, he decided that in this instance he should take a backseat. He patiently heard a lengthy situation report from Sir Winston that concluded that there may be a foreign pilot on the loose somewhere in the vicinity. It was either that or one of the assembled crowd was actually the pilot.

"We had better check them all out," Sir Winston concluded.

Stevens was volunteered for this task, and he immediately began rounding up the guard and hangers on. Sir Winston, in the meantime, returned to his examination of the aeroplane still smoldering in the field.

An hour passed before Stevens felt he could pluck up the courage to report to Sir Winston.

Everyone had been accounted for apart from a young lady and a gentleman, who were last seen heading away from the scene of the crash. Maps and Victoria were in pursuit of the two men last seen leaning on the gate post. Both had imagined that it would be an easy wander over to the gate to ask the two men a few questions about the missing pilot, but by the time they reached the gate the two men had gone!

Indeed, but a few moments earlier Bardufloss and Arnold felt that it was best if they quietly and stealthily disappeared into the countryside.

Finale

It took several days to clean up the mess left by Bardufloss's aeroplane. The extent of the damage to the farmer's field was compensated for by the government.

Maps and Victoria had returned to the camp to find a very annoyed commander and minister awaiting them. When quizzed on their disappearance, a very interesting story began to emerge.

Maps and Victoria tried to find the two gentlemen standing at the edge of the field. Their interest in these two men was the result of Victoria remembering the detail of her previous meeting with one of the gentlemen. The lobster under the coat and the man's interest in the school led Maps to determine that these two men may have had more to do with the situation than they should have.

Maps explained to the two senior men that he and Victoria combed the area for several hours before they concluded that both must have gotten away. After they consulted with the commander's secretary, they got a bus out to the coast and looked for the men there. It was a hunch, but it proved to be a very good hunch.

The two men were found walking the beach in and amongst the rock pools, occasionally gazing far out to sea. Instead of approaching the two men, Maps and Victoria raced back into the town and alerted the local constabulary. However, being a weekend, only two policemen were available to assist in the search. Maps and Victoria accompanied one of the policemen back to the beach whilst the other tried to raise his colleagues from the weekend travails.

Maps and Victoria searched the area where they had last seen the men whilst the policeman walked in the opposite direction to search other areas. After some time searching, Maps and Victoria found the ground very difficult to traverse; the large rocks and boulders that littered the beach weren't to Victoria's liking. Maps sat her down on a large boulder and proceeded to search alone.

Victoria began to relax; the sound of waves crashing onto the shore was very soothing, and the intermittent sunshine on her face was very welcome. She maintained a good lookout, but even if she screamed, Maps would never hear her cries with all sounds of the seaside around her.

After a short time Victoria heard a sound behind her. Slowly she turned to find a policeman splashing around in the rock pools. He explained that he was called to search the beach and asked her if anyone had passed by. Victoria pointed the way, attempting to explain the position of both Maps and the other policeman. The policeman nodded at her and set off in pursuit of the other policeman.

Victoria relaxed once more.

"A crab sandwich, my dear?" a voice from behind her asked.

Victoria turned to see Arnold peering from behind a rock. Arnold approached the nurse cautiously, asking if she was alone. Victoria replied that she was indeed alone. Suddenly, a second man appeared from behind a rock. Bardufloss whispered something unintelligible to Arnold before both men nodded at each other. Victoria was asked politely not to scream or draw attention to herself whilst Bardufloss gazed longingly out to see if his rescuers had arrived.

More unintelligible words were passed between the two men when suddenly from the waves a third man appeared with a small dingy in tow. The little boat was parked amongst the pools and the third man approached. Barduffloss moved forward and exchanged pleasantries with the man before both alighted the dingy and set sail for a waiting submarine in the distance.

Arnold looked at Victoria. A rather startled Victoria looked back.

"It would appear that I am not quite the Gentleman you expected me to be." Arnold began to explain.

"It would appear not," Victoria responded. "You had better have a good explanation for all of this, otherwise I will alert the friends that are combing this beach looking for you."

Arnold paused to reflect and to take stock of his situation.

"I assume you must now know who I am," he started to explain.

"A spy?" Victoria responded.

"Spy is a very evocative expression, I prefer to see myself as an immigrant caught up in an unusual situation."

"A spy nonetheless," Victoria scolded.

Arnold could only agree, however he explained that it was not a situation or occupation he would have chosen under any other circumstance.

Victoria stood and in an action that even surprised her she pointed at Arnold and screamed as loudly as she could. Arnold tried to hush her.

"Please be quiet for just a moment," he pleaded.

"I have information that could embarrass everyone you know and love."

Victoria quietened down.

"Talk!" she demanded.

Arnold began to explain that on his side of the conflict things were very much the same. They also had a secret wood, where they were building a secret aeroplane that was capable of carrying large amounts of troops to the front. The problems they were encountering were the same as your sides problems. In order to win this small arms race they needed an advantage, there for we recruited several important figures.

"The pilot, young Masters, is working for us," he explained. "Supplying substandard rubber components to the factory."

Masters had indeed used his influence in his father's tyre manufacturing business to sabotage the project. He was terrified of flying the new machine and had little interest in getting hurt in a machine that he thought was a crazy idea made real. Unfortunately, the scientists and mechanics at the secret wood were driven to get results by equally crazy officials in the government. It was all a vicious circle and always likely to end in disaster, therefore he reached out and we came up with a plan to destroy the aeroplane.

"But you knew that anyway," he announced. "Masters is a close friend of your own family, and you and he had for some time been lovers."

Victoria was amazed that Arnold knew this. She also suddenly became conflicted. She had indeed hoped that one day she would marry Masters, but how could he reveal a secret like their romance to a total stranger?

"The Cad," she concluded.

"Quite the Cad," Arnold agreed. "It would be such a shame if this news were to become public."

"I have done nothing to be ashamed of," Victoria replied.

A slip of rocks and a crack of broken branches alerted Arnold to the imminent arrival of Maps and possibly others.

"I must take my leave of you quickly," Arnold announced. "Please do not try to follow or stop me."

Victoria sank to her haunches and waved the spy away.

Arnold approached her quickly, pecked her gently on the cheek.

"I am sure we will meet again, hopefully in more pleasant times," he whispered in her ear before he hustled through the rocks and melted into the distance.

Maps climbed over a rock to find Victoria head in hands.

"I heard your screams and came as fast as I could," he began. "Who was that man you were talking to?"

Victoria explained that he was a local fisherman that she knew.

"He made you scream?" Maps enquired.

"He startled me," she explained. "Did you find what you were looking for."

"Sadly no." replied Maps.

Maps explained that the men must have got away and that they were winding the search up.

"Time to head for home then?" Victoria asked.

Maps nodded and placing a comforting arm around Victoria, he led her back to the town and a bus for home.

Review Requested:

We'd like to know if you enjoyed the book.
Please consider leaving a review on the platform
from which you purchased the book.